# YOU GOT WHAT YOU DESERVE

## BETTINA LILLEMOORE

# Contents

# You
# Got What
# You
# Deserve

# 1

## *Dicks*

Finally, I thought, I'm gonna get fucked.

Sometimes it's really easy. Sometimes it takes like forever.

All sorts of shit gets in the way a lot. They've got girlfriends or they've got boyfriends or both of them or they've got political hang-ups against fucking or they've got std's or they're on some frickin religious holiday they don't believe in.

But all around, I'm pretty patient. When I spot a random piece of guy I like, I expect it to put out over time, if that's what it takes. And I understand the rules, the social-political ones that could really fuck someone over if I did the wrong thing. And that's why I waited.

This guy, as soon as I saw him, I registered him downstairs in my little blond sandwich shop, thinking: He doesn't belong here. This guy's bony face and untamed bush of gray hair belonged somewhere else, but not in school. Even with his khakis and baggy sweater on, he had the wrong look for an English teacher. He had the big cock look. Teachers don't have that. They don't because they don't have big cocks. They have puny cocks, puny cocks with a lot of hair mostly. They want to have big cocks, so they work in places that most girls don't know the difference. Most teachers wouldn't survive anywhere else. Anywhere else and the breath of the person you're talking next to tells you how big his dick is. Whenever I talk to a guy, I get up just close enough to catch his breath to tell how big his dick is. Or not. Most girls in high school just don't know about that. And, being high school girls, they hardly know the difference in cocks anyway. So for puny-dicked male high school teachers, the set up is perfect. Christ! Any one of them who brings up in class themes of incestuous sex in *Hamlet* or an old guy humping a young chick in Chaucer seems to girls like it's Mick Jagger whipping it out for his own daughter. *Eew! Don't say that! That's nasty! You mean Nick Carraway is really thinking like that about his own cousin, Mr. Bigdick? That's nasty, Mr. Bigdick, that's nasty!* Sure, even though Daisy is the guy's second cousin once removed and there's like zero blood between them, girls get totally grossed out by Nick having the hots for Gatsby's slutty Daisy and the double or treble ambivalence this causes Nick as narrator slash participant; hence the stifling vocabulary with the mid-western twang. But, truth be told, they love it, girls love it, really, inside their pants. And they love it mostly because of the erroneous fantasy that *Gatsby* isn't clean. Girls who go *eew*!, the same kind who go down on every guy they can but hardly ever swallow the cum, the first to fuck and the last to have abortions, they love *The Great Gatsby* because it is dirty, because they think it's nasty, because they're getting off on their perverted fantasies of Nick wanting to fuck his cousin Daisy. In high school, basically, any girl who's more than vaguely aware that her pussy is more than just of fissure for urination, what they want is to feel the breath of any puny-dicked teacher who'll even say the word "sex" to them. And, as a sort of a whore of the English department, not literally, just an after school flirt mostly, what I learned mostly from high school was that being a high school teacher was mostly all about puny-cocked guys trying to impress the daylights out of hardly experienced girls. And how are the girls to find out or not? The bravest of teachers, the most brazen, who'll slip a semi-avuncular arm around the pint-sized waist of a boppy girl coming back next year for a flattering college re-cummendation, he'll still say to himself and his small dick, "No pair of tits is worth *my* pension." How do I know this? I just know. It's a sense of smell. It's all from learning to catch a guy's breath up close. It tells you everything. And they're all just chicken-shit to show their little high school dicks to girls that hardly even know the difference really, even the whoriest of them. And make it sound like it's an ethics thing, that they can't. It's all bluff. And the teachers all know it. But not this guy, no way. He had a wad in his pants. I caught his breath. I could tell. He was Mr. Bigdick.

It's more than just that. I mean what is a dick anyway? Having a big dick is partly attitude, partly blue jeans. That's where I put more of my energy. The crotch-thing was a lot more reliable than breath-catching, which might really be just a bunch of ballooey. Face it, I myself really barely saw much for dick in high school, so what was I myself to know? Like give-away bikini tops, crotches were everywhere, and the pants a guy wore and the way he swung his legs around, these were the tell-tale signs of who he was and what he'd do or not. Take a teacher in a nice pair of double-pleated slacks, ironed, creased, and cuffed. Kind of boring, but there is that master and servant thing going on there between the teacher and student; it's no *Night Porter*, but, where does the potential for a sex scene drop out? Double-pleats. Any guy, teacher or not, who has to fluff up his lap with an air-bag, it doesn't matter what he's got there inside the breadbox. He doesn't have attitude. He might have the hunger of a bear waking up in springtime, but he's hidden the beast so far back in a dark endless cave of folded cloth, he'll never get out of there. Guys with pleated pants, they're born to dwindle in the background and masturbate. Appetite, yes. Adventure, no. The flip side is a guy in really tight, straight-cut, black designer jeans. When he sits down, it's the mumps, those two gobstopper-sized carp eyes floating to the surface. It's just pure Archimedes. The stuff has to go somewhere. A guy sitting on his desk facing the class with his legs crossed wearing a set of these is making the day for any girl in class out for some pretty gross bird-watching that period. There he is, ass on the desk and, basically, his dick is in every girl's eye, all squunched up there behind that inky black denim. Even worse, when it's so jacked up, like maybe he's shoved a miniature valentine pillow in his underwear, it's pretty obvious that he's wearing bikinis, which means a couple of things: He either wants to be a Calvin Klein undergarment model, or thinks he is. When a teacher thinks he's that, then he's either really in the wrong profession, or there's something borderline debatable hiding behind the stitching of that kind of *rive gauche* wannabe fashion dick hoisted up on the right side there. Bunched-up power-dicks show the attitude of the guy that has to be put up with too; so, if that's the inner-life of the teacher in question, my advice to myself was to skip it. The right look, it's either in a pair of flat-front khakis or a pair of ordinary blue blue jeans. The crotch area, when the teacher's sitting, with one leg draped over the knee of the other, doesn't bulge like he's wearing the mouth of a horse down there, nor cower like a baby bird in the nest

4

when Mommy's flown off for five or ten minutes. It's got the home-made mashed potato look: A good convex scoop chucked between his legs, smooth, with a few lumps. It's the difference between the real pearl, a little misshapen by nature, and the cultured one that wears its shapely perfection like vanity. My taste is for the former, where a guy is cumfortable enough with himself just to be who he sits. It's like make-up for girls — the best make-up being when it looks like there's none at all, or when there is none at all. Wearing underwear's probably necessary to guys, though, like a lens cap is to a camera. Mr. Bigdick wasn't really about size, even though I did think about it a lot; it was about pants mostly.

## 2

### *Bigdick*

*The whole Peloponnesian war can be seen in the ripples of the wall,* he said. And in his undulant pants' crotch, I saw the ripples of my future *till human voices wake us, and we drown.*

Right away, when I met Mr. Bigdick, I noticed his skeptical black eyes set like opals deep back inside his head. Later, when I was in his class, I saw they were never still, always shifting; when he thought, he moved them. He twitched them. I could see, from the second I saw him, that his eyes were alive and thinking. That's a real difference for high school, where most of the teachers' eyes are blurs, blurry circles that look out over the chalkboard walls over nothing, decades of looking over the ash heaps, that's *Gatsby,* too, at their retirement, right over the heads of their students, waiting for their small pensioned ends like a paradise they actually believe in, to come when it finally comes, waiting for it, counting down the years, their lives, they believe, until then dead. And I could see Mr. Bigdick was not like this.

When I met Mr. Bigdick, a little bell went off that told me he was a genius.

I was already talking to Mr. Newcomb, my former favorite English teacher, when he just appeared. Xsu-Xsu and I had been talking with Mr. Newcomb about which courses to take our senior year. He was laughing and laughing, leaning his torso toward Mr. Newcomb, who taught Honors English 9 and Shakespeare; and then me and Xsu-Xsu, eyeing us both. Doesn't even know my name, doesn't know if I talk really like *Me and Xsu-Xsu* or *Xsu-Xsu and I* yet; and, unasked, he's handing out advice to us, no introduction, or who he is, laughing away, in this sort of pretentious definitely not local accent saying: *You should take AP Calc; it looks good; you need the math/science quotient or you'll just look like board-score hackers floating through your own humanistic clouds. Between AP Calc and AP English, it's hands down Calc. And as for Shakespeare, same thing basically.*

He said something like that; I wasn't quoting. That's one thing I learned from him, I'll admit. Narrative quotation is all bullshit. And this guy, Mr. Bigdick, he's like flossing some dumb math teacher's teeth for him because . . . who the fuck is he? Commenting in his totally unsolicited, totally unasked for I'm-the-lighthouse-of-your-college-future solicitous way telling me and Number 1 GPA girlfriend with me not to take his own AP class. Is that what he and Mr. Newcomb were laughing about? And then he's gone. He leaves the room, Cat-in-the-Hat, without a passing introduction or words of parting.

That's when I said, I'm gonna fuck this guy.

My character sketch of Mr. Bigdick would be like this. He was an inch, perhaps two, under six feet, powerfully built, and he advanced straight at you with a slight stoop of the shoulders, head forward, and a fixed from-under stare which made you think of a charging bull. That, of course, is the opening line to *Lord Jim,* which, per his suggestion, I read as my independent book halfway through the year, and it totally fits Mr. Bigdick. Really, though, Mr. Bigdick's strong-guy look, was less physical than Conrad's strong-guy; Mr. Bigdick's was more of a stooped over aggressiveness that was mental more than anything else. He wasn't even big, not huge anyway. But he was powerful. The Mr. Bigdick I knew was Lord Jim powerful. With also his Beethoven hair-spazz thing going, even though it was totally gray, he was like the Lord Jim of the mind.

Maybe it wasn't just like that; maybe the now of the future has distorted the then of the past. Maybe my present emotions are giving fresh tints to what was happening then. Maybe I was sweet. I remember Mr. Newcomb saying right before Mr. Bigdick expelled us from signing up for his own class, "Ah, la crème de la crème" to me and Xsu-Xsu. And then they laughed. Up until then, we'd paid our attentions to Mr. Newcomb, our own sweet, noble, Shakespearean man. And Mr. Bigdick stole me.

The breath-catching might be true or just a bunch of blah blah. It's just a theory anyway, and there's nothing wrong with that.

I'm waffling. I was a junior before my senior year and like a virgin. And I just thought, this seems like a cool guy, I've never seen him before, and he's smart and maybe friendly. I'm not really like at this point: How can I connive, plan, plot; connive, plan, plot to get inside my teacher's who's not yet my teacher's pants. I'm like a 730 in math, and so I know if $q$ is to follow, where's $p$? Where's $q$ if there is no $p$? There's got to be a $p$ to have a $q$. Causal proposition *numero uno* on my checklist of nascent seduction. Where, then, I thought to myself, intrinsically, because, basically, in a sense, I was preverbal then, prehensile, I was like without guile. This was when, really, a thing like innuendo was closer to a literary term than the sandpaper of life.

I owe a lot to Mr. Bigdick. He's the one who taught me that innuendo was sandpaper. I mean he fucked with me, I'm now realizing, and not altogether in a bad way. No, it was good. But it's not always just my own identity that I'm dealing with or even talking out of. It is me. More on that. He loved saying, *Ich bin ich*. I wonder how many other girls he's said that to, too?

Mr. Bigdick's AP class was the most amazing class I've ever had. There were like barely ten in it, and one he drove out. It was a scandal, though he never talked about it once. Talk about taboo. A kid got slammed for internet cut-and-paste. Mr. Bigdick nailed him. Once, the first time the kid did it, Mr. Bigdick, in a decent way, he let him re-do the paper; and the second time, I heard about it, it was Mr. Bigdick cross-referencing the hell out of multiple documents passed to everybody, like a dozen people, including the principal, his parents, his guidance counselor, and two psychologists ready for the kill. It was over for him. The kid got into practically no colleges, and was like over 1500 on his SAT's and, before being failed in the course, second in class rank. The point is Mr. Bigdick knew what he was reading. He knew who we were from our writing like we were world class authors. OK, so it's not hard to distinguish the writing styles of a half-dozen plus teenage kids in one AP class, but the point is that you knew Mr. Bigdick cared about your writing.

I was heart-broken almost the first time that he didn't leave his chicken-shit comments all up and down the margins of my paper. They were runic, cracked hieroglyphics from an ancient Egyptian tomb, and we learned as much about his cryptic ways as we did the literature we read.

Reading Keats, reading Keats' letters and poems back in forth, Mr. Bigdick was like he was him, like he was twenty-four and dying of passion and John Keats' own consumptive end. The class wasn't anything really for three weeks except watching Mr. Bigdick lovestruck with Fanny, reading Keats' letters like he cumposed them, like he was there himself cumposing them. For three weeks, I watched Mr. Bigdick's body rocking back and forth, his harried gray head moving up, and then moving back down. He just got up out of his chair in our circle and almost without a book wrote the words to Fanny with his mouth right there, looking at the wall like the poetic horizon. He went from the letters to the poetry, and from the poetry to the letters. When he wrote about his poetry to Fanny in his letters, sweeping his shock of gray hair back like he was Keats in a sweated fever, Mr. Bigdick showed what Keats had cumposed at the time in verse. He actually made the poetry, wrote it there while he was standing, timing it with his hand, the middle finger of his left thumb circling in so that it touched the inside joint of his thumb, barely looking at the text, timing the lines, his eyes almost closed; then he'd open his eyes and say, as though he was maybe giving us a lesson, *if I can't write a poem as naturally as a flower opens, it's not worth writing at all,* and I really couldn't tell if Mr. Bigdick was talking about himself, as if he'd crossed some sort of personal line of his own life-and-art confession with us all there, which was a little embarrassing, because it was a classroom, or if he was just dramatizing Keats; you just couldn't really tell anymore.

Him tiptoed on the edge of Keats' urn like that, I was the maiden fair Mr. Bigdick was reaching to kiss forever, jerking off to Mr. Bigdick each afternoon I went home after school. I really found that that kind of masturbation helped to relieve the tension before the next class with him again. Otherwise, I just don't think I could have been able to stand it, watching his hands like that, his long, skilled fingers, the hands of a spider spinning his AP magic.

# 3

## Class

Once, he said to me, *Bettina, I was walking through town the other day and you walked right past me. I did?* I answered. *Yeah,* he said, *it was weird, you were walking on the sidewalk toward me, and about twenty feet before we would have met, you switched over to the other side of the road.* My cover was blown and I remember it so well because then Jason, the Jewish James Dean of the class, in his aviator I've-crossed-the-world-blindfolded-in-my-sleep nonchalant way said, *Maybe you didn't see Mr. Bigdick because you were thinking of him at the time.* Vesuvius is bubbling up here, the short-napped industrial carpet with three decades of gum, shit, and candy grit is about to come unseamed. But, quick as a doe on my metaphorical feet, I say, *Maybe I was listening to my iPod.* The comment is so light, so lo-cal lite, so puckishly insouciant that who'd think there was any further verité in what this asshole so soberly pointed out to us all? I'm like that. Skywriting all sorts of things, dandelions, monarch butterflies, baby's breath. But let's face it: Sandy in *Grease* is a repressed whore and I played Sandy. Once, like a century ago it seems, I read a short story that had only one line that I remember: *I want to be good, but misunderstood.* It's a lot like me. I can never be caught.

I don't want to go into what we read; who'd want to hear a litany of texts, as Mr. Bigdick called everything that wasn't live. Paintings were texts. Plays were texts. Musical scores were texts. Sculptures had, text-ure, he said, breaking the dry spaghetti into two syllables. *Life has no texture; life is just protoplasm and then some, stuff without meaning without purpose, without sense, and probably without order. And probably, too, without chaos either. We just jam it into texts of one sort or another, and these relics, these leftovers, becum the texts, or the residuum of consciousness, the echo of the thing that stands better than the original issuer, higher than the voice. The text of Mt. Fuji painted is higher than the mountaintop itself. Without even a cheap paperback throwaway like Into Thin Air, there is no Mt. Everest. It is not about doing it because it's there. That's just plain stupid. By Scott going there, he made the North Pole, and his collaborator, the winky, nature boy totally unsuited for the expedition, Montgomery, he, along with Scott, they deserve the Nobel Prize in Consciousness for making the North Pole. They made it there. As Blake said, the stars are there because we imagine them to be. We are born to make the universe, and without us, there is no pinhole in the cigar box, and without that prick of light through which a photograph is left of the outside on the inside, there is nothing. Not even darkness. We are the nodes of creation, we are the gods of the gods themselves. It takes just one man spinning a pot in Nepal to make the vessel of the universe. With him alone the universe is saved because the universe is made. Without him, nothing. Not even nothing. No antinomies. One pot-maker is all it takes.*

Fuck. Fuck. Fuck. That is exactly how he spoke. It was wild, preposterous, disordered. Like he was my Willy Wonka of books. He was like a reckless genius, but if you listened to his psycho-show, even if we'd mock Mr. Bigdick outside of class on our own by doing the Mr. Bigdick finger-twitch imitations and the Emily Dickinson I've-got-a-poem-exploding-in-my-brain stammer walking down the hall later and cracking up over him, how could you not believe him anyway?

In class it was like being pelted by raindrops, jelly beans, or gumdrops. His words were like a pulse, not hard, but steady like a warm summer rain happening by surprise when the drops are big and spread apart. It was like the sound the sound of a drum makes heard beating through a wall next door, steadfast and sure, like a constant pleasant vibration. When Mr. Bigdick's sounds hit my body, I just sat back and felt them, his pulsating little shooting stars of energy ricocheting off the ceiling and floor, bouncing everywhere and colliding into me. I just sat like I was paying attention to his literary meanings with my eyes wide shut, letting myself feel the waterfall-feel of what he was saying, with his syllables filling the room like heartbeats against my constant beating own, my torso pushed back in my chair by the soothing rhythm of his pummeling voice like the sweet thundering concatenation of horses and sleigh bells, the rhythm of whose hooves trampling the soft snow and ringing felt more like a massage everywhere, in my heart, in my cunt, on my arms' skin when my sleeves were rolled up, and in my shoulders as if he'd walked over and cupped them down and held them back steady with his poetic hands.

Some of the kids hated him. But if he were listened to not as a literary authority, not as a Moses-of-Yahweh type coming down from the mountain with the biggest engraved news of the millennium, if he weren't listened to as a William

Randolph Hearst patriarchal mogul type deciding what information the presses made news; if he weren't dismissed as a quack either with pretensions, or a megalomaniac with delusions; if he was listened to like a little thoughtful and curious kid playing by himself and letting you hear what he was thinking about, dumping out of the wicker basket and then stacking up his wooden blocks on his own with us, and if you built towers with him, and churches, and other buildings with him, it was like an experience no one had had in school ever before. And it never happened anyplace else, even two years later, the way it did in Mr. Bigdick's incredible class.

We read two poems, I remember, called or about being mesmerized. Some kids really said Mr. Bigdick made no sense and was never prepared anyway for class. They'd said his whole style was a ruse, like Hamlet's antic disposition, just getting away with not doing quizzes and tests and normal things like that because he was calling it AP. That's what you get used to in high school.

When we read Robert Burns' poem *Mesmerized* and then Ezra Pound's attributive *Mesmerism*, I was truly in awe. But not by the words even or their meaning. It was what he did with the words, the way he shaped them by shaping himself, grasping with his body, moving, and pulling. Like he did with Keats, he just went into the reading like the words were him. His hands, the more urgently he talked were like hands that were trying to bring down a tense little kite a thousand feet up in the sky, by just grabbing over and over with his bare hands alone the thin filament before him. He was desperately trying to bring meaning down to earth, desperately trying with his hands and his arms and his whole body, I imagined, to bring a lover into himself. And to go back to my kite-flying analogy, it was like he had no spool to wrap his thoughts around; his hands just kept spinning and spinning; they just kept grabbing and grabbing, pulling and pulling. And then sometimes in the middle of it, in like a tirade of words, he'd just stop totally. Nothing had changed except that his body just stopped. He would freeze. His body would freeze, his voice would freeze. He would freeze. He'd just stop there with his arms out like they were already the tree at the beginning of *Waiting for Godot* and we would just watch him motionless ourselves for fifteen seconds of non-moving nothingness, just sitting there waiting for him to start moving again. It was like watching a child watching himself watch sand pouring through his hands; and stopping, realizing what he's doing, and then, after he had stopped seeing himself, going on again, doing something else that wasn't sand now, but something else to him. I know what it was like: It was also like being Dr. Jekyll trying to save himself, who, instead of bolting himself in and locking everybody out, let us in to watch him in his laboratory. And I realized sometimes when I watched him in his classroom passions that I wanted not just to fuck him, I wanted to save him. I wanted to be the medicine that he needed. I wanted to be his poison.

What a loser. I waltzed into his classroom all year long almost, skipping Music to talk with him. Up there sitting on the desk my knees wide open, legs swinging, yakking and yakking away, smiling and smiling. I was the perfect picture of near apoplectic teenage happiness. Aren't English teachers supposed to pick up on that? Aren't they, when a student, a teenage girl in this case, comes to visit them bubbling over with nubile alacrity supposed to pick up on it? Here I am my teenage cunt's practically a yard open, my thighs strapped in blue jeans, my tits as fresh as eggs laid on the farm, and not even a discernable lump in the pants. I mean, Mr. Bigdick, I say apostrophically, if that's even a word, and if not, I am making it, where's the fox in the henhouse? I repeat: Where's the fox in the henhouse? Didn't it ever dawn on him that I wasn't talking about class, that if we talked about class material, it was obliquely, like a sardonic joke, that we were both knowingly playing school in school? I mean, I think the guy's a genius, but for picking up on girls hitting on him, what a retard!

Then, I thought, he's just trying to play hard to catch. This is just one of his chiasmatic reversals, the *minute by minute it changes, it changes minute by minute* sort where he, taking off his vulpine mask, plays the role of the chicken, and I play Ben Jonson. It's a cunt hunt and I play him, a Sadean role reversal. And he scripted it. Maybe. *Puerile sterile Lolita*, he told me, when I told him I'd read it over Thanksgiving and wanted to use it as the book that influenced me the most for my college essay. *Read the real stuff, later on: Justine, Bataille, Kierkegaard, stuff we won't cover here. Here, we're just doing Ivan one brick at a time.*

*There is no such thing as a narrative memory for dialogue,* he said. *When I was sophomore, in college, I burned Wuthering Heights myself in the smoking room of my school's library, trampled it.* And so, when I stopped by 7th period, I didn't ask him about Jane Austen, whom he adored for her depiction of *blunted female genius,* or Brontë whom he likened *to genealogical atrophication in one triad of sisters, the unnamed, the named, the nameless, not necessarily in that order*; I asked him about smoking. He'd smoked he'd said, backpedaling the rectitude of his next comment, like Hiroshima. I didn't know or not what to make of such a hideous comment. He'd rolled his own cigarettes in Hungary when they only had Samsen® and not Drum®, keeping a pack of Camel® straights on hand too. And then we'd be talking not about cigarettes anymore for long, but about Hungary. I was just a young girl from a semi-rural dot on the American landscape, hardly an oasis of culture, surrounded by a bucolic wasteland of rednecks and second-home owners fled from New York. Mr. Bigdick was a gigantic almanac of ideas and things and facts all ripped out and dropped all over the place and I was the construction paper scrapbook of life to have them glue-sticked in. He was a gigantic lighthouse rambling the shores of the world and I was a little girl.

What a dumb fuck. Write in me, write in me, write in me, I kept saying all year; cum in me, cum in me, cum in me, I kept saying all year. And the guy in his weird, self-absorbed, flirting out his guts, detached, and totally fucked-up way barely looked at me. A few times, sure; I come in some Spring days sporting no bra on, my tits like fruit; I spring into class, my nipples jounced through a carefully picked faded orange t-shirt; Christ, I show him my tits, man, and what do I get:

> *Whan Zephyrus eek with his sweete breeth*
> *Inspired hath in every holt and heeth*
> *The tendre croppes, and the yonge sonne*
> *Hath in the Ram his half cours yronne . . .*

And I'm like, don't give me the fucking Middle English, guy! Grope me, Mr. Bigdick, grope me with your hard obsidian eyes at least! Springtide, Yuletide, suicide, the guy was like impossible to turn on. And yet, he was turned on! I bring in fresh-baked teenage tits, hot from the oven, still smelling of the fresh skin of my chest being expanded by overnight growth, the fecund rosemary of the garden rolled between the fingers' smell; my joints behind the knee, lavender; my armpits, lily-of-the valley; my lips, caramel; and my tongue, ginger; and Mr. Bigdick Equinox here feeds me that April with his vertu and shoures sweete stuff and smiles, a smile of April longing, his teacher's eyes just for moment falling down to look at the shape of my bare breasts beneath my shirt.

I figured the guy had to be a pedophile to be that smart and be teaching high school level. Or maybe, thought I, milkweed puff of a girl that I am, I just don't know what really smart people in academia are like yet. Maybe it's just relative and I'll find out next year if Mr. Bigdick is really worth his salt, cracked up to what I imagine him to be. *Why don't you teach college*, I asked him once. *Because I don't have a PhD; you need a terminal degree. I taught some college courses once for a while, as an adjunct, slave-labor wages, and quit when I realized that if I kept taking the throughway to class the cost of the tolls, rather than taking the longer slower back way, was making me lose money.*

I found myself jerking off to him a lot. I wondered, does he ever dump it to me?

Needless to say practically, I got a 5 on the AP. *Read like you're a pervert trying to becum a nun*, he told the class just shortly before the exam in May. When you're eighteen, that sort of shit shakes you up, especially from your teacher. People don't talk like that. Grown-ups don't talk like that. Teachers don't talk like that. And so, it stuck. Of course now in college, that sort of talk is banal. But then, it was high voltage, low amperage stuff. The line worked because we basically were nuns turning into perverts. Now, a professor would have to basically flip the original around: Write like you're a person who has been a nun. Once you have swamswum to the other shore, there is the other shore. I got a 5 partly from Mr. Bigdick's frank brutality, frank only because he decimated his own ranks at the service of his students. *People who read your AP essays are a lot of dopes a lot of them a lot of the time; throw them a hot coal and they have no idea what to do with it. The practice you have learned all year is to throw hot coals. Fortunately, you only have to pick up that hot coal from the ground, that glowing object, that idea that is yours; they have to catch it and examine it. Throw them hot coals and you will score high. Toss them a faintly glowing ember, and you'll get a 3. Throw them a black lump of carbon, you'll get what you deserve, a 2. Even a dope getting paid by the hour over summer vacation knows what a new idea is, but few know how to evaluate the quality of that new idea. Does that matter? Not in these circumstances. The burlap sacks are filled with so much anthracite that Pennsylvania's economy will keep growing at a steady, respectable pace for years, years to come, decades probably, long after the seams are split and the bags rotten. So, it's easy for you, actually. Trust yourself to do something new, and you'll do well. It's really that simple.*

*You're just a better thinker than most of your own teachers, Bettina,* he once said to me. A line like that to a girl who already has a crush on her English teacher is like a proposal to elope. When he said it, though, I knew I had to fuck him.

## 4

### *Cherry picking*

The year was wrapping up. I was off to the Big Apple, practically forced to go to Columbia by him, even though my own first choice was NYU. *Ivy's ivy and 45 grand is 45 grand*, he said. *If you're paying the same fees for club membership, why go anywhere else? And besides, Bettina, I want you to be surrounded by the most intelligent people you can be surrounded by.* That's what did it, actually, not his advice *per se*, but his using my name like that, hearing the sound of my name come out of his mouth like it was inside him always, like my name was born there, and he was letting me have it, like he was giving me a name to go inside my own body to becum me. When I heard my name from him, it was like the whole universe was shut out except for what he was saying, a declension of three syllables Bet-ti-na going from him into me, like I was the only thing that mattered, the only thing that was. So, off to the Big Apple, I invited him to my graduation party. My body, and it's a good one, was wrapped in a silver spangled dress, the dimple of my little cleavage somewhat visible, my white shoulders bared by the garment held up by two silver spaghetti straps. I looked terrific. I watched everyone gladhanding Mr. Bigdick as soon as he came: My bubbling mother, my taciturn father, my nostalgic great-uncle; it seemed, at one point, almost to be a party as much to him as to me. This was due, of course, to my having talked him up quite a bit to all my relatives and friends, especially my mother.

The general party hub-bub changed when Mr. Bigdick sat down on the couch and, from our family bookshelf, pulled down *Little Black Sambo*. Seated on his left already was Xsu-Xsu, the crowned class valedictorian. I sat down on his right. I had not sat beside him casually before. This was not the world of blond, fake-wood desk plastic. This was home, my home. Just then, his tag along nephew, who had accompanied him to the party, popped onto Mr. Bigdick's lap. *Would you like me to read you a story, little girls, little boy? Yes!* we all cried. He read the story, and we all played along with the silliness. I was a little drunk, having had a little champagne, and so horny that I could barely stop myself from leaving and locking myself in the bathroom just to masturbate fast enough to get it over with. Then, the boy on Mr. Bigdick's lap leaned forward to grab a handful of mixed nuts from the bowl on the coffee table; and to stay his balance, Mr. Bigdick held his shoulder; and, in so doing, the backside of Mr. Bigdick's hand touched and pressed against my left breast. He just held it there. *I got them,* the boy said. But his uncle would not let the boy lean back. He held him there, where, I, too, of course, I forgot to mention, had leaned ahead. His hand and my breast were pressed against each other and I felt myself about to scream. I knew I was creaming, I was butter; my half-tried pussy was hot and Mr. Bigdick's big dick was the one cumming. Then, as I leaned back, the nephew munched the nuts down, and the uncle finished the story. I wanted to cum.

What an asshole. I told him that I was going to change my dress. Change dress. Get naked. Fuck me. Here's Mr. Deconstructionist *viva la differencia* who can sleuth out all these mutually incumpatible contradictions denying the possibility of either's textual possibility in the face of reality in the face of reality "*I'm not crazy because I'm not crazy*" kind of Dali kind of woo-woo! kind of guy, and he can't even smell hot pussy when it's right next to him. *I'm going upstairs to change my dress.*

He's supposed to follow me upstairs with several minutes buffer time allowing for conventional discretion. Then, following a gentle knock upon the door ajar, I'm supposed to say, somewhat falsely surprised but invitingly, "Hello? Come in." Then he goes, "Oh, you're changing. I should probably close the door." And, in so doing, he closes the door behind him. Every man worth being a man's got to have a touch of the cad and Cary Grant in him.

This would have been the perfect day. Catullus, to whom Mr. Bigdick did, I thank him, also direct me, lending me an English version cassette tape of the most exquisite love poetry in the world, would have been proud. O Hymen! O Hymen! O Hymen! To give up one's pussy to one's teacher, to be the beloved creamed into above the crowd of congratulatory parents, uncles, nieces, neighbors, old shits, and interlopers, a pretty sister and stranger, by aunts and classmates downstairs — all the friggin Who-ville root-toot-toot noise going on under the stairwell — and to have it bent over, chin down in the fluffy covers, the young girl squealing and her old English teacher heaving, christened proper like a righteous pot-stoned debutante uncorseted ass-up in her little girl's puffy bedroom, getting it good on this day of high school glory by the smartest piece of genius cock you know, that would have been rightly proper, that would have been the entrance royale into the world as we know it, that would have been a graduation gift from Mr. Bigdick to be remembered in life's treasured photo album of super-wows. Those clear juices, the glaucous colored cum, the briny secretions, the reddened blood, the happy, happy tears of Fanny B. and John K., the anointed delicate membranes moistened, the lubricous labia, the bodily unguents, the salves of adolescence and progenitive maturity, this batter of glick and gluck, all this whipped up would have been the fruitful culmination of ten months learning and unlearning, the stitching and unstitching that would have made, in the ah-ah-ah moment of mutual cumming, all the academic labors heretofore seem like naught. Fuck yeah, it would have been great, definitely have been worth it after all.

Witness, then, nonoccurrence of such said event. My perfect adolescence, my perfect adolescent female body held out to him like a rainbow of purity arced across sleeping Neptune's waters of sexual foment and riotous froth; shit, I mean, talk about parody of mis-apprehended opportunities, there he sat, ostensibly imbecilic the whole time eating with his sister's progeny handfuls of party nuts, while I unzippered myself panty naked and, out of sheer spite, did not reach in and kick myself off; out of sheer spite and anger that he just sat there downstairs with his nephew and houseguests like some dumb-ass baggy-sweatered Little Black Samboed white guy happy with a wad of dripping pancakes, sunk there all cushy-cushioned like Macbeth's unwritten, unplayed, unknown twin brother who's afraid to be the loin-balled lion-balled man I did take him for. And there I was. I looked in the mirror, and there I was: Tasty. Breasts like avocados. Avocados resting cool on the kitchen window sill one autumnal day. Breasts ripening before the perfect flesh is eaten; that lovers' food felt by the girdling hand to be both giving and ungiving, having the perfect ripe softness that is a hardness; to have a waist wrapped tight around the pelvis whose sinuous curves are no longer joined to the swing-set bottom that Uncle Jack can without second thought push skyward on the playground to the bright blue heavens, or on the park bench on his practiced knee any longer cumfortably dandle; and a flaxen-haired pussy that, like a yellow-mouthed crocus to the early April sun, has opened itself just a small handful of times in its life to cock itself; fuck, my love was like a white, white mailbox whose hatch still creaked acceptance when the letters came, the paint of virginity not yet scraped off the hinges, my address where my ladyship resided a June bloom hardly found. And he could have had me: Outside the legal spotlight of school, beyond the iron bars of jailbait, in locus familia (that mythically safe haven of all fertile perversions). And he sits there playing uncle to boy and mentor to El Number One in the Class who didn't bother to even take his.

I begin to reevaluate. Is this guy a loser? Short of shoving my pink nipples down his mouth, can't he read the signs? Sign and signified and all that shit. Again, what is the point of Saussure if you can't, as I have said before in selfsame document, smell the smell of hot pussy calling your name? And if you, Mr. Bigdick yourself are playing the tune of warming up my pussy, which you were, albeit discretely, all year you seductive asshole, and can't, when push comes to fuck, bring it off, then what are you doing at my graduation party anyway?

Instead, when I descend, clothed in loose-fitting jeans low enough and a shirt just short enough to show off some lighter hair when I bend to the side just-so, just enough to reach into the Crocodile's mouth before being rescued by the bi-colored rock-snake; instead, when he does get up, he begins a pointless dialogue that, like a wind across a calm dumb lake, kicks up a sudden storm.

It goes like this:

—*Well, you're looking pretty casual there now, Bettina.*

—*I just had to get that dress off finally, Mr. Bigdick.*

—*Well, you look like you're about ready to go for an outing. I went on an outing to this place right around here yesterday, right over the river, on the sunny side, not the gloomy side on which we live habitually; and it was the most amazing beautiful place. It was the opposite of Torneo; it was everywhere I wanted to be in this world, amazingly here. When I was in Rome* [this was typical of Mr. Bigdick; he'd launch off on these asides that seemingly had nothing to do with the topic and without any transition or indicating that he was off and on the beaten path just keeping talking as plainly as shaking salt on a baked potato], *having been invited there by a group of Italians in Cambridge, not the Charles River one, I could, in the morning step out of the back kitchen door and there it was: A lemon tree. I picked a lemon when I needed it. It was like Tuscany; everywhere you looked in this orchard were wet cherry trees, their leaves not covered with dew, but the drops of a shower that had passed, so that the fruit and leaves had a shine, almost like, though it wasn't artificial and tawdry, a lacquer, a high gloss finish, the way milk poured out of a Vermeer pitcher has a static shine of the thing that's in motion actually. A light shining everywhere from the trees and from all of them cherry red cherries. The cultivated pastoral itself. As far as you could see, hundreds and hundreds of trees, trees of the same size as others in the distance growing smaller because they were in the distance rolling over the hillock. And up the trees were these simple wooden ladders, small, moveable ladders to reach the crannies of uppermost boughs, ladders that tapered, narrowing as they went up. And what was the most amazing was, unlike apple orchards where you hunt around and look for the best apples you can, here, every cherry was good. None was bruised or unripe. Every cherry was perfect. I went there actually with my nephew just yesterday, and there he was at the top of a skinny ladder, his hands on the rails, holding out his mouth* [at which point Mr. Bigdick demonstrated with open mouth before me], *reaching for a cherry and, once it was sucked in, surrounded by his lips, his gently pulling his whole body back, not just his head alone, until the small fruit had separated from the stem from which it was being plucked.* [At this point I've totally forgiven him for not coming upstairs to fuck me, and would have pulled down my jeans' zipper there and had him do it] *The cherry season lasts a week, it's only open to the public on weekends. Next weekend I'm not here. How'd you like to go cherry picking with me tomorrow, Bettina?*

*—Sure!* [I answer with schoolgirl enthusiasm]

Maybe he isn't such a chump after all, I thought. OK, the dress thing, and screwing your student at her parents' house at her graduation party might have been a little PG-13, kind of corny actually. But the effect was the same; he caught the fact that I'd gone upstairs, changed, thought about him, and came back down with teacher cock on my mind. He fumbles around making one travel-log digression, trying to get his bearings straight, all thrown off course into total Electro-sexual disarray because I'm wearing a collar-torn dark purple t-shirt that says right over my front in white block capital letters SEE PURPLE? without a bra on. It's a regular Little Miss Muffet and Old Father William dog-and-pony show, and that's what makes it fun.

Before he says goodnight, and he's the last guest to leave, I say out loud in front of my parents that I'm going cherry picking with Mr. Bigdick tomorrow. I say this right as my mom is thanking and kissing Mr. Bigdick goodnight. Then my dad shakes his hand. My mom especially thinks Mr. Bigdick is tops. It's insidious of me, and I know it, but the more innocent I seem (stupid) the more the walls are painted up and down with the clean taboo of white, and the whiter the walls of my childhood seem, the greater the repression of Mr. Bigdick's desire for me. And the greater that desire, then, beyond the outermost limits, past Mr. Bigdick's description of linear perspective, outside the frame of his Florentine landscape painting, at the very last cherry tree at the very outer limits of the estate, I'll be coming down the ladder tomorrow, cherry in mouth, stem dangling. I'll be coming down, wearing a white dress, whiter than white because it's been washed in the fluorescence of Tide®, like Hardy's beautiful maiden Tess, and as I'm coming down the rungs, just before my feet reach the yet untrampled grass, I will feel his bare hands reach, as though to help me down the last few rungs, around my almost virgin hips.

Fucking asshole. He called in the morning to cancel.

OK, at the time, I didn't have the algebra all worked like that. I'm not really all that Jude the Obscure-esque. And I'm not as common, I think, as that bitch with the false pregnancy who did Jude's career in. I just listened to what we were reading in Mr. Bigdick's' class very carefully and listened, also, to what he told us we should read. And I did. People are always telling you what to read, and nobody does. Mr. Bigdick, thinking he was teaching us literature, was handing me his personal curriculum, like a code, that made it really easy to fuck around with his belt buckle. His whole class was about the kind of chicks he liked and the kind of guys he either fancied or didn't fancy himself being. It was pretty obvious.

I was pretty impressed with the cherry picking scheme. I mean, it takes some guts to say to a high school girl, can I pick cherries with you? Mr. Bigdick had used the kind of cheerful briskness that I've pretty much perfected — a practically clueless enthusiasm for the surface symbols, like don't go swimming I can see the sharks' dorsal fins breaking, that are so readable they are the dull and missed ready-made lore of common American culture. But in a master's hand, a cliché well-spent has the genuine ring of a spinning doubloon dropped on cheap Formica® countertop.

Then he just disappeared. All summer long I thought of him. What would it be like to bump into him at Echo Lake? What would it be like to go swimming beside Mr. Bigdick? During the last months of school I'd seen him without his typical baggy sweater on, wearing short sleeve shirts for once. All the other teachers wore short sleeve shirts a lot. Not Mr. Bigdick. Except for the last week. Then I saw his arm, not huge or anything, but well-formed. Distinct veinage on the forearms, the sign of a guy taking care of himself. I knew he was a member of the Lake, and I went pretty often to a catch him July and August. I think I saw him once, pulling out with two boys and a woman with him. I was jealous enough to drown all three of them, and for a moment I was disgusted with myself for wanting to suck the dick of a guy that old when I saw her. Not that she was awful or anything; she was just like a wife, and that looked really gross. But I was never really sure that it was him. It just made me think, mostly about me. How could he have gone to Echo Lake with her, with her middle-aged Volvo-proper face, and have canceled going to the cherry orchard with me, me who was the hobgoblin of milk and honey in size five panties, me who was fresh and inexperienced and ready to move my legs and arms anyway at all, ready to try to learn whatever he said to get us both off together, shit, just thinking about it made me horny and angry; and instead to go with some leftover mother who's been having sex so long that fucking was like grocery shopping for the family for them. Yuck! And I was alone. I was new. My pussy'd been gone into, honestly, like twice. Yum. I was Yum. Yum-Yum.

# 5

## *College*

Mr. Bigdick ignored me all year at college. I wrote him a letter in the fall, just rambling on about shit and school, and how I was going to use him as my verbal ash pit. I don't know why I called it that: Ash pit. What a prescient little whore I turned out to be! Next year, the WTC was torched and voilà, it was the perfect excuse to call Mr. Bigdick. I mean everybody was connecting with everybody. Nobody needed a justification to call anyone. If you knew somebody from second grade, you googled them and called. So what? So I called up Mr. Bigdick, leaving my cell number. And he, since I had left a message, called me right back. He was very professional. I told him all about how I'd just gotten out of the shower and heard the planes flying overhead, and saw them flying, really just one plane, and just watched out the bathroom window in my towel, which I'm sure Mr. Bigdick was stifling a perversion over. I mean how many people were even thinking about fucking at that time then? Me and Mr. Bigdick were, I can tell you. Sure, it was nasty and tragic, but just calling him up to see if everything was OK for him, without really a sensible reason why it shouldn't have been, the touch of cumpassion by a teenage babe like me in a wet, pale green towel wrapped around her body on Mercer Street peering out the bathroom window of some boy's apartment overlooking the Washington Square Park arch; that kind of capricious attention from a young whimsical girl caught in uncertain circumstances who, wrapping herself up in a towel on the phone, to see how her old English teacher is doing ensconced in the Berkshires alone when the whole neighborhood is a mess of smoke and ash, that's good camouflage for the erotic. Except for this one returned phone call, in spite of several handwritten letters, he didn't call back that year.

That didn't stop me. On Spring Break, I went back to the high school. He saw me in the hallway and, doing his best to keep his teacherly demeanor, hugged me in the middle of it. Who'd have known I wasn't a student, not there anymore? He couldn't resist me. And why not? Well, because I was dressed in my new groovy way showing some skin, looking a bit grungy, a bit I've just crawled out of sex and cigarettes, even though I hadn't had either that day. But, shit, I knew what Mr. Bigdick liked. As I said, I spent a whole fucking year studying the guy. One of those growing up in sixties guys who like Schoenberg, Glenn Gould, Leadbelly, and Nirvana. So, in I walk, swaying my little hang-down tits like Janis Joplin's. And what does he do next? Immediately, he sweeps me into the some obscure dingy office without a phone or secretary. I think this is it, finally. I'm gonna get fucked. It would be perfect. There's a long cheap table, a corkboard with flyers thumb-tacked into it from what looks like fifteen years back, and then, for no reason except to make me know that there is one, Mr. Bigdick ducks into this little hidden bathroom at the back of this back-alley office. Again, I think, perfect, great: He's gonna get me to go in there and finally, finally, we'll fuck. I'm so excited thinking he's gonna fuck me. It'd be fun; I mean, right in my old school, with my old English teacher, Mr. Bigdick. I mean, that'd beat even the eight mile high club, doing it with Mr. B. while he's at work. He's a genius to do it here with me. And, again, it happens: He starts in on college. He starts in on curriculum. He starts in on my major. Oh, he's self-ironic about the banality of his inquiry; it's not like Mr. Bigdick doesn't know what he's doing. No, you take a guy like Mr. Bigdick and he's just the opposite of the Charles Manson type: No blood and mayhem, no movies are going to be made after him. There's no crime, no clues, no evidence. It's just this devoted teacher conversing with his former student, having a conference just like the old days, only the door, as a graduated student now, can be fully shut. The words just aren't the words. He knows it and I know it. Nevertheless, while I'm thinking about how much standing-up room or not there is in the back bathroom, and if he's gonna do it my palms to the walls or my ass up against the plaster, and if I can keep my voice down, because when I fuck I'm almost always noisy, I'm talking back to him about Camus, and I'm talking about Sartre, and he starts talking about Blanchot, Maurice Blanchot, and Kafka, and *du* and *ür*, and the first-person as writer, and oh my fucking Lord. I'm totally juiced for it and the fucking guy chokes. And I know, I know it's total bullshit, and what I want to do right there at the shitty old dirty long table is take off my shirt and show him me. I want to show him I'm beautiful and not just his student. Look at my gorgeous tits! Look at them! Look, I'm not your student anymore, my pussy is screaming so loud I want to cry.

It was another whole year after that.

That year, without Mr. Bigdick, was amazing. I really had a lot of sex. I drank a lot, went out to clubs, learned to drink Drambuille. I got into anal a bit, not that much, just with a few. I did drugs. Before that, in high school, I never touched them. I really was an angel. My favorite thing to do was read Thomas Mann up in my dorm room with a real kerosene lantern alone with a bottle of Riesling in a t-shirt. Of course I was reading *The Magic Mountain* because Mr. Bigdick had said it was the greatest novel ever written. *Finnegans Wake shall have been remembered, but The Magic Mountain will be known. The best thing to do is to find an apple tree in New Hampshire, climb up it, and read the goddamn thing.* Yeah, I read it, during the winter with my window a crack open so I didn't die of fumes. Not an apple tree, but alone. I had a little fake sheepskin rug that I'd curl up in and with my t-shirt pulled over my knees like I was pregnant look-ing, I'd read *The Magic Mountain* all night. I usually did it without even panties on; and, as expected, masturbated a lot in between, not the chapters themselves so much, but the little abstracts, the introductions Mann gives to set up his chapters. When I got to the French part between Mlle. Chauchat and Hans Castorp, I had one hand in my cunt al-most the whole time. Shit, God, Fuck! Mr. Bigdick was right again! It's the best. The truth is, no matter what, I couldn't get away from him.

I just had, I said to myself, to fuck him, Mr. Bigdick.

And then he called me. He called me. I repeat: He called me. It was a little queer, actually. He asked me if I was going to be in the neighborhood over the summer or was I keep-ing my place in the city. Then, when I told him, he told me that he was going away for the summer, for the first half. *Shall we get together when I get back*, he asked. It made me a little nervous. He had called to tell me he was going away and would be back? Of course I understood later that it was a push-and-pull strategy. He wanted his and my whereabouts to seem merely a matter of course, but really, he was pinpointing the moment when we could be alone together with no other personal interferences. He was collecting data. Playing dippy, I asked him where he'd gotten my number from. *Your post-WTC letter; I keep it right next to my bed,* he said. *Where you keep everything important,* I asked. *That's right; you gave me your email, too, Bettina. Which do you prefer?* When he was on, he was on. And, honestly, I was a little bit scared now with his calling me anyway. It was too exciting. He had talked about his bed and I gave it right back at him. My handwritten letter next to his bed for a year was like me sleeping there in it. And true or not, he was telling me how he felt about me, that he wanted me. It was even better, I thought, if he was making it up. He had waited two years since my having been graduated from high school for the whole saucy pedantic wretch of the world to get out of his eyes so he could make love to me, so he could fuck me and I could fuck him. I could tell now that we were going to do it, that he'd cleared everything for me, that he'd spent two years doing it, making everything look right; not in high school, nor too close to high school because he was afraid; contact, but not too much contact. It was all pellucidly clear to me now. In his mind, just the right amount of time had passed to make his calling me seem a proper enough distance. Poor Mr. Bigdick, I realized, had spent all that time quite unnecessarily restraining himself. From day one, I realized, as long as I'd been thinking about him, he'd been thinking about me. As long as he'd been thinking about me, I'd been thinking about him. I masturbated as soon as he got off the phone. And I was sure he was too. After I came, I thought, yes, poor Mr. Bigdick; I would have fucked him when I was his student easily at seventeen. He could have done me like a ready-made virgin if he'd wanted it. And I'd practically been. And I'd be a Duchamp for him now if he wanted it; if he wanted it like a schoolgirl's who's barely felt cock inside her, I'd let him open me up and fuck me like that now.

After cumming, I saw that Mr. Bigdick was and always had been cumpletely in my power. Always. He was always mine, and I was always his.

In Van Gogh's painting with the crows flying over the field, there's a big difference in seeing that painting as just another great Van Gogh and seeing that painting knowing that it's the last one he painted before he killed himself there. I'm hardly the suicidal type, but it dawned on me like death's flock of dark feathers, thinking back to Mr. Bigdick's lesson on John Berger, that maybe what I thought had been obvious from practically the start to me hadn't been obvious. What if the signs I thought I was giving that were obvious were not obvious? It's all about how you see things, and in what context. *Context is everything, and I tend to regard each plait, each feminine braid, as its own delimited totality. That's just the kind of reader I am. When I'm looking at Tess' hair, which is what I'm talking about, I'm feeling the filaments of Hardy's own risqué fingers. The worded residue of his slow, ineluctable fondlings are what literature is. It's just dust, really. But where else can a person run her finger along the path, the channel, the groove, like a needle vibrating in a record, in the traces of a first-rate mind? Maybe in music.* That's more or less a summary of what he said and some of Mr. Bigdick's literary philosophy. It's a scary thought to think, though, that maybe everything's that's obvious to you is only in your head, in your own context, and that nobody else can really feel what you're feeling. Scary to think, I've thought, that what I felt wasn't ever felt also by him. And even though I thought I was being pretty obvious, what if I hadn't given Mr. Bigdick the faintest suggestion that I wanted to fuck him, and so, he never knew? What if to him I was just painting crows?

When I met Mr. Bigdick for the first time, he was already talking to Mr. Newcomb in Mr. Newcomb's classroom. I didn't knew who he was, some teacher. They were laughing heartily when Xsu-Xsu and I came together to talk to Mr. Newcomb about which courses we should take next year. Mr. Newcomb, who really is the sweetest guy I have ever met, did say, *Here they are, la crème de la crème*. And I thought, does he mean Xsu-Xsu *and* me, or just Xsu-Xsu, but has to say both of us because both of us had come together? Xsu-Xsu was ranked first in the class, became the valedictorian, and I was, even though I was pretty high up there, nowhere near that. She was smarter than I was and, half-Asian half-Hungarian, even prettier. She was everybody's absolute favorite. Her eyes were the type of Chinese eyes that looked right into a guy's mouth that said to him: *If you should be so successful as to win me, you can put your penis inside my mouth and I will, sealing my lips around the pole, swallow every gram of your cum while looking up at you to see if you are happy with my oral performance*. If her tilted eyes had been on a billboard, every guy who liked girls would either be veering off the BQE onto the rumble strip or running away from his life to becum a sign painter just so he could get his gluey hands on the paper strips of her blow-job eyes pasted forever into the minds of millions of other men driving by. And yet, there was nothing seamy or nasty, there was no sarcasm; there wasn't even the wafting incense of irony in her. She was the good, the true, and the beautiful. She should have been called Agatha; that would have been perfect, not some half-whore's name like Xsu-Xsu. Xsu-Xsu's name was her only irony. I didn't really resent her for who she was; she was my best friend. But with her basically Asian looks, which were smoothed out so she looked like a whole different species of the ultimate beautiful and traces of her swallow-sounding Hungarian accent, even though her English was native-speaker perfect, she stole the show. She had always stolen the show. Between two girls, who was Mr. Bigdick, not knowing either at this point, going to notice? Not me. And who was Mr. Newcomb, whom I did adore, really looking at? Her. And did I say, *Thanks, Mr. . . ? Thanks for the free advice! I'm Bettina Lillemoore, by the way.* No, I didn't. I had not. Against Xsu-Xsu, with her clichéd porcelain skin, tawny fresh as the lotus blossom Chinese lips, and the fact that she was like 5'8", was dressed in a black pashmere sweater that showed off her little Chinese candy-plum tits, I was positively scrappy. I'm not, really. But beside her, what was I to look at? And I did nothing to place even a white foot forward.

I let the whole thing go actually.

Next fall, like the first day of school practically, by total coincidence, Xsu-Xsu and I ran into Mr. Bigdick in the hallway. *You are both missing out on everything's that's happening!* . . . And I'm not going to even tell it, but for a good fifteen minutes he went on and on about AP, as though he expected us to have known who he had been last Spring and what he taught. And he was the same as those first feelings I had about him, only it was more powerful. His uncut almost crinkly gray hair shot out almost like he'd been electrocuted in a cartoon; he wasn't like a freak; or have that *Maybe I am-Maybe I'm not Einstein-at-the-tiller of the sailboat, or maybe, universe look*; or that bored genius look of: *I've already seen through the pane of glass look and I can tell you that it is for the most part clear, yes*, look. He was just his wild, regular antic self. Xsu-Xsu was mature, presentable, and graceful as always and expressed her dismay over not being able to take his class because of a scheduling conflict with AP Bio and how in college she wanted to study rural agronomy in the Third World and how AP Bio was in her field of intended interest as well as providing balance to her transcript for college, to Princeton, where she was applying early. And then, he looked at me. *What's your excuse, Bettina, are you applying early to Princeton, too?*

That line changed my whole life.

What made me drop AP Calc and take AP English was his knowing my name was Bettina. Sure, he'd remember our faces, especially Xsu-Xsu's, who wouldn't, but I hadn't told him my name. And it hadn't come up when we met in Mr. Newcomb's room. There had been no introductions. Only Mr. Newcomb knew who everybody was. Mr. Bigdick had had to have found out on his own. Maybe he knew who Xsu-Xsu was, maybe he didn't. Who didn't? It was nothing special. What mattered was he found out and remembered me.

# 6

## *Getting stoned*

Part of the thing was I liked other English teachers besides Mr. Bigdick. There was Mr. Newcomb, of course; and also Mr. Lederman; and Mr. O'Casey, a really nice guy I'd had in seventh grade, before he switched to the high school. They were all great guys and I was a busy little bee many an afternoon visiting them, all four sometimes. Mr. Lederman, that's Jewish for leatherman, was the only one who ever said horny-sounding things to me, but he was so cool it didn't matter. He was like in his sixties already and could get away with that kind of shit. *Get out of here, you little she-devil before I smack you somewhere where it might just feel good for both of us!* He'd say something like that if I lingered too long in his classroom after school and he wanted to go home or correct papers. That never bothered me. Mr. Lederman, I swear, he could have dandled every girl in all his classes on his left knee with the fluorescent overhead lights turned off, whispering sweet nothings about Prince Hamlet in their ears and not one of them would have said a peep to anyone about it. He was just a great guy, and all the girls in his classes came to him like ants to honey. I was just one of those favorite ants. And Mr. O'Casey, another guy I loved, who because I'd known him for five years already, from when I was just a little girl really in junior high, and also because I babysat for him, he was more of an old friend already that I could eat at a barbecue with with his wife and kids and it would be normal as the neighbors, because he basically was my neighbor. They were all cool guys. And I loved to hang out with them.

To him, my hanging out with Mr. Bigdick could have looked just the same. In a way, I did hope it did because I wouldn't have wanted to have made him uncumfortable. That's bullshit! I wanted him to notice me, but I didn't want my other teachers to notice. Also because they sometimes would say things. *Hey, Bettina, I noticed*, Mr. Lederman actually said to me once, *that you've been spending a lot of time lately with Mr. Bigdick. What's he got that I haven't?* I was mortified. But that's just how Mr. Lederman was. Horny. Still, I tried to keep some balance. Basically, if I did spread things out with guys I really actually liked, then my hanging out with Mr. Bigdick more, it wouldn't really look like anything. Since their doors were all like right to each other's, it wasn't like they could pretend things that weren't. Sometimes, I'd be in Mr. Lederman's class swinging my legs after school, and Mr. Bigdick would walk by and give a smile. Other times it'd be the other way around. So even though I skipped a whole semester of Music to visit Mr. Bigdick, and we never talked really about anything we were reading *per se* in class, he could have taken it as totally innocent because he'd seen me, English department whore that I was, spreading my swinging legs everywhere else, too. But I really wasn't a whore. I wanted to find out about Mr. Bigdick and his mysterious past. Mr. Lederman had already been an English teacher for about half a century; and Mr. O'Casey I already knew for half my life. Mr. Newcomb had also been at the high school forever and was just like Shake-speare himself, which he taught, anyway. Mr. Bigdick could have been a spy before, or should have taught college, or a mad scientist, but whatever that mop of bushy gray hair was, teaching high school was more like a great accident he'd made than a plan.

I don't know what I want to do, I told him. I think I'm going to be in school forever, for the rest of my life it seems. I know that what I do I want it to be something dramatic. But I don't know what that do part is.

*The only thing worth studying,* he said without blinking, without even a glint in his eyes like he was saying a foot is twelve inches, *if you're not taking hard sciences, is Classics. What I did in school, really, a joke. Here I am, my fourth year and I'm a discontented anthro major, whoopee, which, incidentally is always the major of choice for valedictorians; you never see a chemistry major as valedictorian, because anthro is easy, everybody knows that, and I decide to switch to English. It's already November and the lichen is shrivel-ling up on Marie Louise La Fontaine's gravestone where, I shouldn't say this, because you are after all a student and I'm supposed to be a positive role model, not to mention that I am, in fact, a government employee, who, in his con-tract for employment signed . . .*

*Just go on, Mr. Bigdick. I don't mind!*

*Well, Bettina, in the middle of winter when Hanover re-ally sucks, I'd get really stoned, which I shouldn't say, why do I tell you these things . . .*

*And?*

*And sometimes like that I'd go out to the graveyard where there was a little girl's grave with pictures of lambs carved into the granite, little rococo sheep, sentimental curlicues in* perpetuity, but worst of all was a picture of Marie La Fontaine's blond little face just as she was at five forever, in color. And I'd lie down in the snow with a Walkman playing something like Gang of Four, who incidentally quote right out of Conrad's Heart of Darkness, We live as we dream alone, or the Psychedelic Furs, really stoned and sink into the snow in front of this grave at night, with this convex memento mori, like a brooch — and what was I saying?

About switching to English and Classics, I think?

Right, so I switched to English, when it was just getting cold in Live Free and Die New Hampshire, where if you're under eighteen the signs indicate that you must wear a helmet but not if you're over, and I decided to bail out of anthro and do English. So, my to-be advisor, the silver fox, they called him — "And then, the next thing you know," he'd say about Stephen Dedalus in Joyce's Portrait of the Artist as a Young Man," looking down and closing his eyes at the podium, doing a slow whisk of his silver hair with one hand across his brow like this in front of all the a-goggle girls in the front row; and then, looking up he'd look at us and say, "is that all of a sudden he's smarter than we are" — this guy I loved gets slammed by some chick, why am I telling you these things, he'd had a fling with who later, after they split up and she was back together with her previous boyfriend who'd been failed subsequently in Mr. Boston's class, my beloved professor; she brought out all his hand-written letters — awful — and Boston — who to my knowledge has never published a word since — was kept chained like a half-dead bear to the same associate professor post for the next fourteen years because of the little, well, vindictive bitch. And so, when I waltz into his office in the middle of November announcing my plans, after taking one course I *got, I must immodestly admit, an A+ in, he says, Bigdick, if you graduate this year, it'll be the greatest miracle since the raising of Lazarus. Which I'm embarrassed to say I did, and with top honors to boot. How? I took about twenty-four feet of books, measured with a tape, from two libraries and for a month read everything on the syllabus. Anybody who can polish off a major like a greasy bucket of Kentucky Fried Chicken is pointing out major problems with the academic system. But, shit—*

*It's OK, Mr. Bigdick. I'm not ten or twelve. In January, I'm going to be old enough to vote.*

*The point is don't study English in college. It's a waste of time. Apart from the hard sciences, which are a good way to go, study Classics. Classics will teach you how to think.*

That would be a 7th period.

Even if he was self-aggrandizing or even if he monopolized the conversation, he was amazing just to listen to, the way he would drop and pick up what he was talking about and even though it seemed pretty chaotic, he maintained a point, focus, actually. He was the most roundabout talker I'd ever known, but, even though he'd talk about really nothing but himself for forty minutes, he was giving me a lesson, giving me certainly an unorthodox delivery, but when all was said and done, that went straight to my question. He didn't tell me what to do; he taught me by using his own life experiences as examples — not like everybody else in high school who professed to know answers, and to give really straight-sounding answers, answers to life that didn't sound like they'd tried them themselves, and if they had, they had reduced their experiences to multiple choice options A, B, C, D, E for themselves even, worst of all. Mr. Bigdick had not.

His thinking was alive, fresh. He was real, and I felt he genuinely meant to help me.

I loved his stories. I wanted to be in them.

It was also kind of weird though. Not the references to his being in college and smoking pot. That didn't bother me. But when he did that swooping thing with his hand and his professor, I did have my doubts. What I didn't do, though, is jump in and say *Is that supposed to be an analogy to something?* I didn't because I didn't want to give myself away. The story was about what to study in school, not about a professor broken on the rack of academia for an affair that back-fired. That was tangential, I said to myself. Or was it? Maybe the whole thing was warped to look like Mr. Bigdick was helping me decide my academic future as cover for his being just a lecher. I didn't want that either. It was confusing.

And he did help. I'm a Classics major.

And he actually did do something that shocked me. He told me one day not to come by 7th period anymore. He was nice about it, smiling, and polite. But he ousted me.

I tried. The: *OK, Mr. Bigdick. I'm not ten or twelve. In January, I'm going to be old enough to vote.* I had meant him to notice that I wasn't a child, that I was almost eighteen. Because I was born late in the year, or early, depending if you're talking about the year year or the school-age year, I was almost the age a freshman in college would be. If I were at college, then, as an adult I could do whatever I wanted. He and I could have done whatever we wanted. Right. So, the only difference was that I was practically at college but I was at high school. And AP, technically, was a college course. Which made me think if by his telling me the story about Mr. Boston, was he in his own deft way warning me? Of course, the consequences of a high school teacher getting caught having relations with students is basically life-ending, in terms of jobs, I knew that. In my town, he'd be tarred and feathered down the Mississippi, or in my case, the Hudson. And before the issue of our relations even could have really surfaced between us, it was like Mr. Bigdick brushed the topic and me right out of his free period. Except, that he did say, *Come by anytime you want after school to talk, Bettina.*

Really when I said: *It's OK, Mr. Bigdick. I'm not ten or twelve. In January, I'm going to be old enough to vote,* I wanted him to treat me like an adult, and fuck me like one. That it was OK to fuck me because basically I was an adult. That was the point I was making. That's really what I wanted him to see. And that's what I'm unsure about if he ever heard, ever noticed, or ever paid attention to. Maybe my points were so slight, so small, especially beside the gushing torrent of his mind, that my desires were unnoticeable.

# 7

## *First sexual encounters*

The first year of college was actually sort of traumatic. *I'm much more interested in where words come from than what they mean now*, Mr. Bigdick said once. Yeah, right, trauma, German. Thanks for the etymological note you sounded in my searching soul, Mr. Bigdick. The year it began that way, traumatically, and got worse. I was going through the shopping catalog, the face-book of all the available freshmen, and circled this one guy's black-and-white head. He was kind of dorky looking, and I liked that, with a distinct Adam's apple, not bulbous or anything, not a *Cat and Mouse* bobber of a thing, just prominent. His hair was longish, looked sort of probably blond, covering most of his ears. He looked kind of spaced out, actually, not like he was posing for a photograph, definitely not yearbook handsome, as Holden Caulfield puts it. I imagined he was a math genius and played bass, not electric. He was like the anti-Uncle Sam poster that looks directly at you from every direction. He, with his probably pale blue eyes would never look right at anyone. *I'm gonna fuck him*, I said to myself. And then, like the second day of orientation at some typical Columbia mating ritual extravaganza, I met him. We talked and he asked me if I wanted to go see the peacocks, which I thought was pretty funny, being in New York City. And so we left and went to the park, where, scraggly as the pair was, prowling like beggars, were the actual peacocks, the very same that the august Pharaohs used to use to sound alarm around their palaces. They were dingy, especially the male, with his half cement-scraped tail feathers dragging behind him like corn stalks that need to be thrown out after Thanksgiving. I saw the bluish and greenish peacocks in the fading Manhattan afternoon as the gloom descended, which, to me, an upstate girl, was still in its incongruous reality absolutely fabulous. Then he made an allusion to Argus, which I let slide by. We were both a little drunk and made out in the scrappy park. And then I took him back to his room, a single dorm room. We were making out there when he said, *Should I get a condom?* And I said, *Sure.* When I came by again the next day to his dorm he was busy talking to some guy down the hallway, his pale blue eyes, which they were, looking elsewhere. He didn't stop talking to this guy. I just hung on the wall for a little, them not addressing me. Then, I just sort of said *hi* and asked him if I could come over. And he just said to this guy he was still busy in the middle of talking to, *Gotta go,* like they'd get back to their important subject when he got back later. I took off my pants and stuff, but not my shirt or anything, and I did him again. Then I told him that I'd been a virgin the night before and he said, *Really, I didn't know that.* Not that I was expecting him to say anything like, *Oh, would that have made a difference?* or *I wish I had known.* He wasn't callous; he hadn't said, *That's cool.* It was just some makeshift scene between us that just happened. And that was the end of it.

The next one was from a philosophy class I started and dropped. He wore a crumpled Filson hat that he said brought him luck. This was the only actually humorous thing he said that I didn't laugh at. In fact, that was the only thing that was funny that he said that I should have laughed at but didn't. I laughed because he was very fine and handsome, especially in his olive Filson, and said many things I didn't care about anyway. Turning it around and around between his hands at a diner before putting it either back on his head; or, as co-incidence would have it, down on a table at the Hungarian, which was, of course, right across from the cum-polluted fountains of Morningside Park where stalked the inelegant peacocks, he played around with his father's old hat. And, in between our getting hysterically jerked up on cinnamon coffee, I did him for about a month. He told me that he'd never fucked someone he hadn't loved like he fucked me. He didn't care a whit about me. I hated him and myself.

I thought of the difference between these regular boys and Mr. Bigdick and wrote him a letter thanking him for being a mentor and a friend. He was, I wrote, besides my own parents, the most influential person I had met in my life.

Then there was Dylan Thomas. Besides Wales, he had obviously picked the wrong place to go to school, being cracked on *ad nauseam* with endless cheap shots over the bard's spewing his guts at the White Horse or dying like a roach in a puddle of spit at the Chelsea. But he hadn't gotten into any other Ivies; so he was forced by his family to weather four years at Columbia. He couldn't help it, he was born to be pretentious, and was a literary pervert. He read to me from Milan Kundera, cajoling me with a greased up copy of *Slowness* in one hand, and a clean glob of Vaseline which he fingered into my anus with the other, before sliding up his enormously long but not too thick Baton Rouge uncircumcised dick. It wasn't the fact that he preferred my asshole to my naturally lubricous cunt that bothered me, after getting used to it it's a lot of fun, but Dylan's getting off while reading to me from the aforementioned *Portrait* itself, another heavily inflected alcoholic masterpiece, about a boy's wet dream that told me it was time to move my pussy on. If he liked that sort of shit better than me, better than the real McCoy, why bother with the guy?

Moving right along, I met a Dutchman, an older man downtown one night at a club, the Jersey infested Nest. He was like a beautiful angel stretched out to six foot seven. Every time he came, he broke down and cried on me. Once his cum was in me, he cried and cried and muttered and muttered. He explained to me over the weeks I allowed him to fuck me every night practically about his being afraid he'd becum a paunchy alcoholic like his father, and especially his being afraid of his inability to love women. That's what made him cry on me, he said. He came, he cried, he explained. Then, after all that, he'd clear the wet Dutch boogers off his soft blond face, and thank me in a polite and quiet diplomatic voice for sharing my body with him. We listened to Verdi together from like a dozen black mini-speakers mounted high up in the corners of his tin ceilings. I liked that. He introduced me to Rilke's poetry, doing him in German and doing him English. I liked that. He ground by hand fresh coffee beans for just one serving of coffee apiece in an aluminum hand-grinder that was bolted into an enormous practically twenty foot long butcher block table. I liked that especially, too. But I got tired of his colossal fits of mourning and ritualistic gratitude and stopped visiting his loft. Even though the place was gorgeous and he was some émigré with not much else to do except pick up college-type chicks willing to strip while he jerked off, after I got used to doing that, too, the attenuated European freak got to be a bore. Cry, cry; thank you, thank you. Like a cultured automat. It was then that I made a vow: *No more guys whose fathers are alcoholics.*

A couple of days out of the parental nest and I went from voyeur-poseur to balling guys whenever I got the chance. Shit! what was happening? The more cum that was squirted into me, the more I forgot about my high school fantasies. Where, I began to forget, where was Mr. Bigdick when I had needed him? But it was great now. I was cumming like a banjo. A dick'd slide in me and I'd just work it, work it till it made me happy. Sure, I'd crash sometimes when I sat down at a class and my ass was sore, wondering if I were overdoing it, overworking the famous ninth portal of God. But I loved it while I was doing it, and met all sorts of guys and they were all pretty smart, too, not just the usual crowd of kids I went to school with. I ventured everywhere, and really fucked everything. All races, like black and white, hispanic and asian. I put them in pairs of races like that in my mind, like things that don't go together but often are. And for different reasons that were all basically the same all the guys dug me for their own. White guys liked to do a white, blond middle-class girl because I was so normal and pretty; black guys into their American history liked the race reversal effect of turning on the little white girl; some guys felt like they were polluting me, some felt like they were touching a fucking goddess. Whatever. Everybody has their own culture's fetish to play out and I could play the role of any and all of them. Just for who I was, I was having a blast. It was everything I dreamed the Big Apple would be and more.

So maybe it wasn't so bad. Thank God I'm the kind of chick who has orgasms when she's getting fucked or I would have felt like just a whore. I can't imagine having to go through so much sex and not getting off on all those great boners.

When I said good-night to Mr. Bigdick the night of my graduation party he gave me one thing before he left. I forget to mention it. Maybe. My parents were on the porch. I watched my mom hug him and kiss him and then my dad shake his hand. Then I blurted out about going to cherry orchard in front of them tomorrow, and he made a kind of inchoate froggish sound. The kid was inside collecting the *Star Wars* trilogy I'd given him that no one had ever played even once. And then Mr. Bigdick, just smiling, walked off into the dark without saying anything. His nephew came out with the tapes and said, *Where's Uncle Enright?* And I told him good-night and that his uncle had gone, I guess, to the car. Mom and Dad and I were cleaning up stuff on the porch when Mr. Bigdick came back alone. *It's a little corny, but corny is best.* He gave me two things in fact: Yukio Mishima's *The Sailor Who Fell From Grace With The Sea* and, written in Mr. Bigdick's pretty illegible handwriting, a poem. The novel was an old Bantam 55 cent yellowed paperback classic with the little red rooster on it. On the inside cover was the signature of E. Bigdick '65. That would have been Enright Bigdick; Mr. Bigdick was Enright, Jr. It was his father's book, originally from his own father's bookshelf. I thought immediately that it was special. And written there on the inside flap was the poem in Mr. Bigdick's trademark green ink:

> *Western wind, when will thou blow*
> *The small rain down can rain?*
> *Christ, if my love were in my arms*
> *And I in my bed again!*

And then curly-headed Mr. Bigdick looked at me, not shaking my hand, and just said, *Good-bye, my friend Bettina. Good-night, everybody.*

That night I went upstairs after we had finished cleaning up, put my face in my pillow and cried. Maybe, I thought, Mr. Bigdick wasn't a genius; maybe he was just in love with me. Maybe what I had heard from him all year was that. And, being my high school teacher, it was choked in him. He had of course to choke it. And I lay there like Desdemona. *Nobody, not even the rain, has such small hands.* Yes. Nobody, not even Shakespeare knew Desdemona was crying. She was crying in her pillow like me while Othello's hand pushed her down. But that wasn't Mr. Bigdick. There wasn't any hand. There wasn't any Iago. There wasn't any force, none at all. There was the gentlest man I had ever known. He had told me he loved me and good-bye in one stroke. He had been the perfect teacher. And I realized then that Mr. Bigdick was really always more to me than just my English teacher. I realized basically what I always knew. He was my life's way, he was my lover, and I had just missed him forever. And that, painfully, painfully, was what he had prepared for me all along. He had just let me go like he was supposed to; but I did not feel, as I was crying, that I could ever ever him. I felt like I was Dorothy at the moment when she actually wakes up back in black-and-white Wichita and realizes with all the gratitude in her heart like a manic explosion that she is exactly where she belongs and always had been and always wanted forever to be. She just hadn't realized the love she felt for and from others who were always there. And my heart broke the opposite same way, realizing that I was exactly, however much I loved and truly did cherish my parents, where my heart now was not, and worst of all, as my recognition got blacker and as it got blacker clearer, that I could not with Mr. Bigdick ever be. I had just lost him now. I just cried and cried all night face down on the night of my graduation; I'd been masturbating and cumming almost every night since I was eight, and this night I didn't for sure. Love would never happen in this world. It just couldn't, and I knew it then like forever.

# 8

## *LSD & Creativity*

*Wagner! Wagner!* That's what we were playing what we wanted to play louder. Our arms around each other's waists, standing on the windowsill together, we screamed *Wagner! Wagner!* The music was already turned up all the way. We screamed it out together, looking out over the sidewalk to make it louder. Every time we screamed it, we couldn't hear the music. And so we had to get back to hearing the Wagner. When it had to be turned up louder, the whole thing started up again. Since our door was wide open, a boy came in to turn it down and when he did, we screamed together the same thing *Wagner! Wagner!* And when he left, we turned it up to the max. We held a discussion about the open door. Without knocking, he could get in. How could he get in by knocking? Knocking? And we laughed, crouched together in the windowsill four stories up. When he came back, we knelt side by side, pressed our cheeks together, and watched this boy. When he left, we forgot about him. Every time we screamed *Wagner! Wagner!* we screamed it both at the same time. It just happened that way and was the best thing in the world. The November sky was filled with me and Daria, and Wagner and was the best thing in world. And we had left the music going by leaving the door open, which made sense at the time. If Daria hadn't screamed *Wagner*! the second time, I had to jump. And if I hadn't screamed *Wagner*! the second time, she had to jump. Then Daria got the idea that she was going to fly. And I got the idea, after she did, that I was going to fly with her. We got stuck on the idea of what we were going to wear. We tried and tried to figure it out but it was too difficult. We wanted to fly but we couldn't figure out what to wear. What to wear really became the problem we couldn't solve. The whole idea about flying out the window together, which we had wanted to do so badly, fell apart.

*Mr. Bigdick, did you do, I know I probably shouldn't be asking this, and you don't have to answer if you don't want to, but did you do a lot, or any other drugs when you were younger? You don't have to answer if you don't want to. I just think from the way you talk, and I don't mean it in a bad way, I really don't, you just seem to be freer than most other teachers I've had, most other adults actually I know; not that that means other drugs, I'm not saying that, but that you seem more open to experience than, well, most other people are. So maybe that's what I'm talking about. I'm always trying, not always really, but I'm trying to put together your life, I mean it seems like it's so, ugh, rich, that you've had all these experiences.*

*Well, I could object to the question, your honor, as to form. It's a two-part question, at least.*

*I probably shouldn't have asked it. I'm sorry.*

*Don't be sorry. You haven't done or said anything to hurt me. You're just curious. I always thought that that was a good thing. What's to be sorry for? Nothing, Bettina. You needn't be sorry for anything. My basic attitude, and I don't know if I'll talk about myself, though I probably will, I can't help answering you, especially knowing the tremendous* sacrifice you're making of your future musical career by being where you shouldn't be right now—

Do you want me to go?

No, no, it's OK. Just watch it. I'm not sure what to do about it.

It doesn't matter. I get a hundred there anyway, so it doesn't matter. It really doesn't.

So — Sise! Sise!

What's that?

It's just, Shit! Shit! in German. Which I don't, by the way speak. Pound says nothing in German of any worth has been written in five hundred years; so that's one language off the impossible weight of becumming a poet. Not one language out of the fourteen or so he recummends a person needs to have read to becum a poet. It's the attitude of Robert Graves, another well-trained, well-educated poet.

Do you think of yourself as that? I mean the poet part? I'd like to be a poet maybe, or a writer, something creative. I can't see myself doing anything practical, not practical in the usual sense. I'll probably be in school forever, if I can help it. Even though I don't know anything about it really — after all, I'm not even out of high school yet of course — I think being a writer is the best thing a person can do. It just makes so much sense to me. It just seems like the right thing to do.

Bettina, I wish this were later. I mean I wish this weren't taking place here and now; I mean, I wish I just knew you; not like this, because there are things I don't feel cumpletely cumfortable saying; I mean, it's pretty stupid that I'm supposed to cow you off to a class that you don't need to go to anyway, but that's what I'm supposed to do. It's the institution; and I am, after all, part of that. And what am I doing? Talking to you about my drug history . . . either smoothing out the cake's icing or declaring, what, the cake has no icing;

*or telling you something closer to the truth that in the sugar-laced frosting there's some pretty hairy white-water, and I don't disrecummend licking the spoon, but that it's not for everybody?*

*It's just a conversation. I don't think you're telling me to do anything, Mr. Bigdick. I'm not going to take it that way anyway. It's just a conversation we're having.*

*One of these days, I'm going to kick you out of here.*

*I know that. Just tell me when you want me to go. And I'll go. It's OK, it's really OK.*

*I'll tell you what I say to most teachers, and you know how I am.*

*Yes, I know how you are, Mr. Bigdick; that's one thing I can say I know.*

*There are two kinds of kids. Kids who do drugs and can handle it, and kids who do drugs and can't handle it. I don't think there's any correlation between kids who do drugs and do poorly in school, well, maybe there is. There's a correlation but it's not causal.*

*What are you talking about?*

*Kids and drugs.*

*But I'm not talking about that really, Mr. Bigdick. I'm talking about what makes you creative. You're the most creative person I've ever met in my life. I don't know anyone who looks at the world the way you do, and I want to know how to becum that.*

Mr. Bigdick had no idea what to say to that. He stopped and looked down at his hands, looked at his long fingers to find the answer there, his long piano playing fingers. And he couldn't find his way. I could tell that he was lost. He was stuck. He looked down at his hands as though if they didn't give him what he wanted to say, they were going to be axed off the next second. Maybe I had embarrassed him. Maybe I had complimented him. It was like he'd been playing spidery music his entire life and he had never heard any of it, which was kind of strange considering how he always pushed us to think wildly, or, as was his favorite saying, *to shoot from the hip*. Mr. Bigdick always shot from the hip; that's what was so great about him, and about me, actually; that's just how I am naturally. I'm a naturally shoot from the hip kind of gal. His very opening words to us were: *In this course we will challenge the banality of orthodox thinking*, and when someone questioned his pronunciation of *banality*, we went on for about ten minutes about the immediate and irretractable social effect each variation of *banal* the speaker will have willfully or arbitrarily created upon the mind of her listener — substituting the feminine, as was his custom, for the standard him or *the deadly duo of him and her, and never, unless you're parlaying with a linguist, or a political candidate trying to garner support from everyone say 'they' when you do mean one or the other;* and about code-switching between the dialect accepted as Standard, at one time just as aberrant as any other English dialect, and any other equally eligible outré patois; and even though there was the impending death of the oblique case, and even though me and Julio down by the school yard certainly sounded better than what he called the Apartheid equivalent of Julio and I down in the courtyard, he'd opt us only for the latter; and the difference between an approach to language that was prescriptive and descriptive; and because of the ineluctable reality of it all, language would not, in spite of the well-meaning sandbags schoolteachers tried placing around it, blow us out of the trenches; that we were all the living carriers of its evolution; that as hosts of what William S. Burroughs called a virus from outer space, like mold on bread, we were its carriers and its agar; and how, still, each moment of language is an extreme moment of personal and political betrayal, and on and on and on, all year like that. Christ! Mr. Bigdick could make talking about a grain of sand alive, but he himself, and I found it pretty ironic, was uncumfortable with being called creative. When I said to him that he was the most creative person I'd ever met, he looked like that idea about himself hadn't crossed even his own brilliant mind. He looked down at his hands like he was the first prehensile guy who when he saw the late afternoon's beams sunning across a river parted his lips and says aloud: *Path of gold*, and doesn't quite yet get it that that is like humanity's first moment of poetry, of creation, of making. Straight from the *Poetics*: To call something what it is not, what I learned from Mr. Bigdick himself, was the essence of metaphor. *To cumpare, not!* he screamed at us in his revolution against the American academy of public education. *Not cumparison! It's an injection. Genius consists in the swiftness of apt perception to come up with new metaphors. And I don't care what it's in: In language, in numbers, in visions, in all media — to have the daring, the temerity to call another thing what it is not; to slip the totally wrong glove right onto what might not even be a hand for all I care and for that wrong thing to fit perfect; tight is tight; it's just tight: Marie! Marie! Hold on tight! To dare to eat a peach, to be Cinderella waltzing in ski boots!* Even if I was basically a child to him, which is what I basically was almost then, I felt that my telling him about his being creative was actually my telling him something about himself that he really needed to hear. And those beautiful hands of his, spinning their rough magic. Gosh, had he been my Prospero and I his Miranda, I would have fucked him just for those ten callused fingers alone. I was his snow-white Cinderella; he just hadn't realized that yet.

*Creative? That's how we all are. People, as I see it, are either opened up or closed down. And people either help open other people up or assist in closing them down.*

*So that's why you became a teacher? To open people, as you call us, up? I see myself as a professor someday, if I'm not a writer, or both. That's the only way I think it's possible to "open up" for me.*

*It was a way of saving myself from, well, closing myself down.*

*You're not closed down at all, Mr. Bigdick. That is the last expression I'd use to describe you. You don't know what closed down is. But do you ever see yourself, and I don't mean this in a bad way either, because you really are terrific, just the way you are you are, of being somebody famous?*

*Why do you say that?*

*Because you're an incredible teacher, I guess. And I can see you being something else. You're not like other teachers I've had, not at all.*

*Haven't we just reversed roles? I'm supposed to be encouraging you to be, to becum. Which discussion is had in the Protagoras, Plato, and you should read it. It is the text where the beauty of all deconstructionist hell breaks loose, by the way. If you're not becumming, you're a dead man. It happens to people: They wake up, and one day, when their journey's half done, they say: Here I am in a big dark woods. It's the middle of my life. And I'm entirely lost. Then, they don't move. They just stay, lost in the woods. Not moving is the mistake.*

*I'm lost now and I'm only eighteen, well, almost nineteen. I'll be nineteen in January. That makes me old, for my class,*

*I mean. Not for you of course. I hope that doesn't mean I'll only live to thirty-seven! Not even forty! If I'm lost now, where will I be later? Because I am lost, I really am lost, Mr. Bigdick.*

What he didn't do was move over his seat next to mine. What he didn't do is console me. What he didn't do is assure me that I was wonderful, not to worry, that everything would be all right. What he didn't do is say cumforting things to me. What he didn't do is lay his hand on my shoulder to assure me his earnest support. What he didn't do is look at me to see if that was OK. What he didn't do is slip his arm tenderly around my back. What he didn't do is reach his hand around my other shoulder, giving me the chance to cry. What he didn't do is give me a chance to lean my head against his supporting arm. What he didn't do is give me the chance to nestle my head against his sailor strong muscle. What he didn't do is get up out of his awkward desk beside me. What he didn't do is, standing, his bulgy denim crotch above my eyes, above my mouth, reach over and touch my hand with his fingertips. What he didn't do is raise me from my desk. What he didn't do is stand me with his hands. What he didn't do is lift me with his power. What he didn't do is look at me with caring eyes. What he didn't do is transfix me with his gaze. What he didn't do is embrace me in his arms. What he didn't do is tuck me in, allowing me to cry in his chest, and I to drape my light-haired arms loosely around him. What he didn't do is give himself the chance to wipe away my tears. What he didn't do is let himself wet his fingers with my trickled tears. What he didn't do is let my tears fill the swirling canals of his fingertips. What he didn't do is let himself taste one of my sweet tears. What he didn't do is let himself mix the precious salts of my body with his. What he didn't do is let the fluids of our two independent bodies join each other. What he didn't do is let himself gently hold my face between his caring hands. What he didn't do is give me a chance to look at him and smile. What he didn't do is give himself the chance to smile back at me, allowing him thus to move the clumped strands of my tear-moistened blond hair out of my face. What he didn't do is let me bite my lower lip and tremble maidenly. What he didn't do is let our flushed pulsing lips open and close, open and close. What he didn't do is let us breathe each other's air. What he didn't do is, inches away, let me glance down at him, bashfully checking out his pushed out crotch. What he didn't do is let himself, in turn, glance downward at me, checking out the nervous rise and fall of my small white breasts. What he didn't do is make my rose nipples stiffen and emerge and press hard against my blouse. What he didn't do was touch the pink of my breasts pointing to be touched, to be seen, to be tasted. What he didn't do was pull my body against his. What he didn't do is feel my pelvis crushing into his. What he didn't do was cram me into him. What he didn't do was take out that fucker. What he didn't do is pound me against the wall. What he didn't do was let me see, let me look back up at him and smile and him smile back at me. What he didn't do was let us smile at the same time to show that we knew that we had just smiled in turn at the other. What he didn't do was let himself put his hands loosely over my shoulders and look me once more in the eyes, one last time, and for me to smile back at him that it was OK. What he didn't do was let the next thing happen. Fucking Mr. Bigdick: I'm right in front of him, I'm there for the asking, the grapes are hanging off the vine, and he doesn't pluck. I say: I'm lost, and Christ, he can't do it! I'm lost; I'm lost; I'm lost! Find me, Mr. Bigdick! Find me, Mr. Bigdick! It can't be that hard! Don't you know English? I was so revved up I thought it was impossible for him to do nothing. But Jesus H., the guy just couldn't. I wanted to run out; I wanted to cry; I even wanted to smack him; I was so frustrated. I was so horny, my cunt was so slick by then that if he didn't do something I knew I had to get to the nearest girls' bathroom to jerk off right away just to finish it or I was going to lose it. Either he had to do something now, I thought, or I was going to have to reach in there, there and then in front of him myself, just to relieve the awful tension of him just totally dorking out on me. He could have done almost anything: He could have run one finger down my arm, from my shoulder to my elbow; it could have been barely sexual; he could have nibbled the eraser of a pencil and looked me in my left eye, (that really gets me off when a guy does that left eye thing), and I swear I would have cum on the spot in my sky blue plastic seat.

It wasn't me who was lost. It was that fucker. I didn't need to be any Xsu-Xsu with her flat little Chinese whore tits, with her perfect cross the t, dot the i personality. Every teacher was creaming after her. Xsu-Xsu this, Xsu-Xsu that. Xsu-Xsu that, Xsu-Xsu this. Who the fucked cared? Not one of them would touch that Tupperware vagina manufactured in China. I was the one who would do it. I was the real slut. I was the real pussy. I was the real lay. I was the real girl. I was the one who, with her real legs spread apart like a yardstick, would have squatted down right over Mr. Bigdick's succulent face and let him lap up the trickling clear juices of my sweet little teenage cunt with his tongue right up there inside my tiny dank teenage hole you could barely get a pinky finger into. And the fucking fucker continued to lecture me.

*You're lost in the best way you can be. You're perfectly lost, Bettina. You're exactly on the path, and it isn't the one* that leads to the Arnold's Bread Factory. In order to get lost in the woods, you have to be in the woods. Not everybody goes there. You can get just as lost in a bread factory as you can in the woods. But you have to be in one place or the other. The thing about bread factories, though, is that they're pretty safe places even to be lost in. Everyone has a place: One man, one job. A niche for every person. Blah blah black sheep. There are bosses, workers, machinery, systems all in place and the future is just as predictable as the past. The present continuous is safe; yesterday is the precedent for tomorrow's probable prediction. Blah blah black sheep. Hume doesn't even hold that the Sun rising tomorrow is predictable; but he just annihilates the functioning of his own reason as he reasons — brilliant self-sabotage. The woods, though, is a different, special place altogether. It's unpredictable, paths are uncertain, nonexistent. Strange little women want to put you in cages and devour you. Wolves appear. Grandmothers disappear. It's a world of illusion, mystery, truth, foreboding, deception, shifts, soothsayers, and stutterers. The woods is the world's own magic drug, and you're in it. You don't really need anything else; the rest, the other stuff, it's just special effects. Why bother? You're just as liable to fall into a vat of dough in a bread factory as you are to fall into an unseen chasm in the woods. That's I how see it.

I'm as good as an angel. I really am.

I know that.

And kick me out he did! That fuck Mr. Bigdick must have been on to something; he must have been on to me; he must have smelled something. What was he worried about, that I'd tell someone I was fucking him?

Boy, I missed those seventh periods with Mr. Bigdick! I really missed them. Going to Music really sucked.

## 9

### *Wonder & Invention*

Come to think of it, I wonder what it would have been like, really. I mean, the guy was no spring chicken. Mr. Bigdick had the name all right, but did he have the machinery? He might have been one of those guys who pump you and pump you and pump you, c'mon pumper, c'mon! but never cum. It's not like I've never been with old guys before. I was fucked by this old Navy guy, I don't know why I did it. It was just for fun. To get done by a fat old guy who'd had his glory days about a million years ago from whacking off some Japs or some Korean dudes now doing my little hardly used-up twat, what a bang! I mean, I know it's sort of disgusting and all, but that's what I like about it, this old guy thinking he's so lucky and special getting to do me. Guys my own age, they never really feel anything so special about doing me. They hardly if ever notice what a tight little clean unbabied cunt I've got because they're after all in the same boat of cum as I am! Guys my own age, they don't send a dozen roses the next day. I'm lucky when I get a "what up" the next time we run into each other on the sidewalk. That's just the way it is. I've got nothing against it. It's my generation, and I like it. But it is nice to be thought of as special, even if it's corny and old-fashioned by some fat

old gook-killing Republican slob who's got the guilts fucking me so bad he sends flowers to make himself feel more
like a gentleman than the pig he actually is. Guys my own
age, they never make me feel like a lady. An old pervert, I
get a little loud at a restaurant with him, bang a wine-glass
with the back-end of a table knife for sport, and he says,
really patronizing, putting his fat old fingers soft on top of
my wrist like they're pressure points or something, *Bettina,
that's not very lady-like of you.* It shows he cares. I like it. It
means I'm noticed and beautiful, and I like feeling like that.
Old guys, they really give it to you. I think they're the best.
Except the cumming part. They go on and on, doing their
humping routines, making it like they're doing it for me, you
know, for my sake, the not wanting to shoot their globs of
mulchy yogurt up inside me thing before I myself am ready
to cum, that whole sensitive man act old men do, when I've
already buzzed it up alone without all their mattress-slap-
ping hoopla about it about three times, good ones too; and
at that point, I'm just waiting for the woo-hoo of some old
lady's husband to be over and done with it inside me. Young
guys, who cares if they cum on the spot. They're like cap
guns. They keep firing. Bang! bang! bang! They're not like
some freakin Brahms symphony that just keeps building and
building and building and building the same symphony it's
been building and building and building for the same hour
it's been building and building already for ten hours straight
that by the time the crescendo comes, you're so sick of hum-
ming the tune that began in the first bar, you just want to
get the freakin melody out of your head. You just want it
over. That's what sex with old guys is like. I can't imagine,
though, that that's what Mr. Bigdick was like. He was so
*Julius Caesar*, he was so Cassius, with his lean and hungry

look. I mean there was the whole *Tess* thing that happened, right? It's Tess, *Tess of the D'Urbervilles,* the quintessential white-trash meets bourgeois guilt-tripping upper-crusty melodrama, Mr. Bigdick called it, where right in the middle of class Mr. Bigdick gets up out of his seat, walks over to me, and right there, right in front of everybody, well, like all eight of us, right when Alec pushes a plump ripe strawberry right through Tess' pouty half-reluctant mouth, like ten pages before he rapes her in the dark, Mr. Bigdick gets up and with his bulgy flat-front khakis standing right in front of my face he pops his finger in my mouth. I couldn't believe it! I think everybody was stunned, me included. *What does he do?* he shouted. Nobody said a word. *What does he do, I ask?* he said. Nobody said anything. We just looked at him. *He rapes her!* he cried. *He rapes her with a strawberry! He rapes her with his fingers,* he cried, *just like this!* And this time, he squeezed his fingers together like he was holding something, like prongs, like those shiny robotic egg-beater prongs reaching for a cheap little fluffy toy in an arcade coming down to grab it. He pressed his strawberry-squeezing fingers together like a shiny robot and pushed them in through the air like he was going into Tess' mouth. And then he said it: *Is not the act of oral sex the same as vaginal sex except one is at one end of one tract and the other at another? Is not Alec performing oral sex on Tess? And don't you think,* he said, *after he force-fed the strawberry to Tess, don't you think he licked his fingers? Don't you think he licked them free of her spit?* And while he said this, he licked his own, licking what was my spit off his own one finger. *The question I want to ask you, though, is is it rape? Or is Tess herself somehow responsible, culpable, involved, participatory, engaged herself?* he asked. *Does not every woman who opens up the possibility that a man might approach her sexually, being that she is woman and knows from her birth what being woman entails, through both nature and nurture, does she not put herself willingly in a dangerous situation which with foresight and a lack of desire to be engaged by a man she might easily otherwise avoid? Bettina,* he said, with my mouth dirtied by the chalk cleaned off his finger, *what is the position of Tess in society, as depicted by Thomas Hardy?*

*Verbatim.* I swear it. Who could forget it? You don't just forget that. We knew right then that we had a real pervert on hand. We knew right then we had a madman. We knew right then we had a genius. And I knew right then like what you know you want what you know you want when you ask Santa Claus for it what I wanted. I wanted Mr. Bigdick's big dick. I wanted it inside me. It was slippery. It was wet. I felt the first drops of the Exxon Valdez oil spill spilling on the shore of my desire and longing. I felt the lurching slick of emptiness wanting to be filled. I felt as I parted my knees somewhat, the stick of moisture sticking. I had felt Mr. Bigdick's long skinny finger inside my chalky mouth. I don't have any cavities. My teeth are like glass. His finger had touched them, scraped them dry. I wanted his big fat mooch, I could smell he had a big fat one, inside the folds of my fire-engine red fields of virgin femininity. I wanted his cock.

I couldn't keep it to myself, not that class. I told that slut Xsu-Xsu about it. Well, I don't know, she said, it sounds like his metaphor is overwrought. Xsu-Xsu went to Harvard, not Princeton, an absolute idiot. Not everyone who goes to Harvard is, but she was, I have to admit it. She had the emotional core of an ice-ball, not icy like cold, not icy like holding back, not icy like heartless, not icy like malevolent. Icy like icy. Like nothing there. Like no feeling of

Wow! in her soul. You take an old Greek bastard figuring out the mass of an object and its relationship to the volume of water displaced and stuff like that, and when he figures it out, he goes like *Jesus Fucking Christ*! Or in Greek, *Eureka*! He goes screaming through the square half-naked to everybody: *I found it! I found it! I found it!* He's got a hunk of some metal in one hand, and another barely holding up his toga and he's running around like a Greek madman telling everybody what he's figured out. The same is true for Einstein. The guy gets a paper published, his first one, and for five solid minutes he's flapping his elbows and crowing like a rooster for five minutes straight. *Cock-a-doodle-doo! Cock-a-doodle-doo!* In Jewish German of course. You can't even imagine Descartes like that. *Cogito ergo sum.* You can't even write it with an explanation point, that's what I like calling them myself anyway: Explanation points, because they explain how happy you are, or how much trouble you're in. *Verboten*! See, it explains it. René Descartes: Totally ice-age ice-heart. No fun. Isaac Newton, I think he was like Einstein probably. You don't just drop stuff from a building, watch it land and smash and don't go, when they crash at the exact same time, even though one object weighs like a hundred times more than the other, *OH, SHIT*! The best are *Oh, Shit*! kind of guys. And while Xsu-Xsu was a Miss Practically 1600 Club kind of girl, she was about as much fun as a sterling silver piccolo stored in a purple velvet carrying case. I'm telling her how much I want to be humped by Mr. Bigdick, and she's saying his metaphors are overwrought. Who talks like that, who thinks like that? People like her, they'll uncoil the coils of the human genome backwards and forwards and figure out how to make every incipient dwarf embryo with low-I.Q. probability into well-groomed parted on the left-hand side blond Nordic tri-athletes who are able to solve linguistic riddles in their second tongue. They're the ones who'll figure out slicing bread and packaging it; they're the ones who figure out on which side of a matchbook it is best to place the strike-pad; they're the ones who figure out how long the length of thick metal chains of swings at public parks should be; they're the ones who'll figure out the odds of survival and are disturbingly right; they're the ones who forecast and predict the interdependent complex of human activity — social, political, and economic. The Xsu-Xsu's of the world are usually right about everything. They go to the best schools, have the best jobs, have the best incums, make the best spouses, have the best children, and so on. They are the intellectual infantry of total human boredom, though. They don't fuck. They don't get mad, really. They don't get pissed. They don't get jealous. They're usually understanding, cumpassionate, and realistic on the sunny-side. Overwrought! I'm telling Xsu-Xsu this guy, Mr. Bigdick, is coming on to me, he sticks his finger in my mouth in class today like it was my pussy right in front of everybody! When it happened, I blushed like a whore taking off her stockings in front of who turns out to be, whoops, her own father stripping off his undies for his own daughter. Real unlikely case scenario, but anyway. The total bulgy outrageousness of it, of him, was he wasn't even secretive. It wasn't like I had to go to him like the cliché-crush for help on my English paper or, *Could you read this poem for me* that I wrote that's all *The Rocking-Horse Winner* about an adolescent girl thinking about fucking an older man and *Can you tell me if you think it's any good or not?* No, he came right out in front of everybody and basically dropped his pants and said, OK, Bettina, Blow me! Overwrought, my ass. I told her: I think he's oversexed, actually. You don't have to take it that way, she said. Besides if he were, she said, using the subjunctive to show that even though she's first-generation English-speaking Chinese she can speak the language better than most white people in Congress, don't you think he would be more prudent? With a name like a whore, I could see Xsu-Xsu was going to have three bonny Amerasian children going to Wesleyan, Tufts, and Yale in a Volvo.

How could that fucking bitch have turned out right? Maybe, is it possible, that when he had asked me to go cherry picking he meant cherry picking? You take like the oldest corniest symbol of a girl's popping her cherry and the English teacher asks her to join him to go cherry picking the day after practically graduation: She's no longer his student, he can't lose his job, she's eighteen, and he means actually to just go to an orchard and pick fruit? My little beehive gets all buzzed up for the bear to rip into the honey-comb and it's no dice? He actually just means a summer outing with his former AP student, me? How insulting! He is about to show me a piece of displaced Tuscan paradise in Greene county and all he means to do is pony up the dollar per pound of pick your own? It's insulting. I hate being white and good. I hate it. Let's say I was that bitch-slut Xsu-Xsu. He'd have had the crowbar in the trunk ready for her, I'm sure. She'd have done what she'd done in every class I had with her that year only worse, unbuttoning her little white Chinese blouse lower than Liberace's naval, flashing her little Chinese pancake tits that aren't even tits without — because it was summer and so hot — even the skimpiest fake little I'm-not-really-a-bra little Chinese bra on. They can do that, and get away with it, Chinese sluts, and still look ladylike instead of the sluts they are. What a fool I was! Like he even really ever wanted me in his AP class. It was all a ruse. All year. It wasn't me he wanted. It was her. No, it was she, nominative, fuck, I hate all the shit he made me know, he wanted, not I. Not I, said the pig. Mr. Bigdick would not have canceled out on Xsu-Xsu, that's for sure. He'd have put an appointment to rotate his snow tires ahead of me. For Xsu-Xsu, that son of a bitch would have carried a parasol through Death Valley over her flat-faced head. No doubt about it. I hated being that Chinese bitch's second fiddle. They're always always first violin. My Irish-German breath, forget it. Flute music? Embouchure. He couldn't care less. For Xsu-Xsu's jasmine exhalations, though, bolts of volcanic lightning dashing the muddy ground at his feet could not have stopped him. It was stupid of me to have invited her to my graduation party. Inviting me to the orchard was just an angle to get closer to her. That sly mother-fucker, I hate him. That's why he canceled. He couldn't get closer to her. I hate Mr. Bigdick.

Not really. How could I hate you? Ever. You who told me the truth in *Lolita*. You who told me, the conventional perversions in Nabokov's masterpiece, a failed writer who wasted his top-tiered mind writing narrative limericks instead of another *Karamazov*, which was more his speed than being the Russian Groucho Marx of mid-twentieth century American literature, of having intercourse with a minor and murder, these are mere novelistic gimmicks, you said; no, you said, the real tragedy, which, because of the success of its gimmicks, is hardly ever heard, hardly ever seen, because it is the gimmicks, you said, that draw the prurient crowd to lap up *Lolita* year after year, and never, you said, underestimate the power of the prurient and tawdry in American letters; the sad truth of *Lolita*, Bettina, you said, Bettina,

Lolita, you repeated, see, you said, it almost rhymes, is that Lolita, Bettina, never loves Humbert. Humbert is mad about Lolita, crazy about her. But she is callous. She is after all, just fourteen. Ouch! She's pouty and precocious and she, well, just doesn't care. She's fourteen, how could she appreciate a mad genius like Humbert Humbert? How could she, Bettina? You tell me. I want to hear it.

All that finger in the mouth stuff about *Tess*, that's me talking shit. In reality, he pointed. I'm really mad though. He just as well could have. It's practically the same thing. He really did kneel before Maureen, yuck, what a stupid name, but not me. He knelt before her and did the Alec strawberry-in-the-mouth-thing. Of course he didn't touch her. Or me. He was so gung-ho about Thomas Hardy, he was such a literature freak, I don't think he saw anything else when he did Thomas Hardy except Thomas Hardy. You'd think he would. You'd think he'd read between the lines. *Verbatim*, yeah, I wish he'd been.

I'm just so unhappy about it. I wasted my whole senior year because of him. I was just too afraid, I guess to do anything about it. I mean, supposing I'd asked him to do something with me, and he says no? His therapist lived right down the block from me, and I could have said, Mr. Big-dick, can you give me a ride home when you go to your therapist? To him, therapy was like a multi-vitamin for the privileged class, and everybody today, he said, lives the life of the privileged classes. Look at the clothes we wear, the cars we drive. We talked about everything. We talked about Brooke Shields during seventh period once, this was before that fucker kicked me out of it, and he said, I shouldn't be saying this, but I will, I don't know why, I don't know why I tell you these things, Bettina. I loved how he hooked my name onto the end of a sentence like that, with a comma, Bettina, like that. And I remember he said, when Brooke Shields took her panties off in nineteen eighty, the separation between the upper and lower classes went fffft! The middle was gone. My Mr. Bigdick would have gone a lot further than that. My Mr. Bigdick would have said: When she took off her panties and put on her Calvins, her pussy was for everyone. Brooke Shields, he actually said, became the dream girl of the American Everyman. Since then, the middle-poor of America are just as eligible to be driving BMW's, he said, as the Dartmouth elite. There's just no distinction anymore. And I'm thinking, when he said that, I want to be your Brooke Shields. I want to take my panties off for you. I want to be your American pussy. My Mr. Bigdick. My Mr. Bigdick would have skipped therapy. He would have come right over to my house. I would have been his therapy. I would have been his Brooke Shields, his *Blue Lagoon*, his amour Parisienne. We both know French. We would have spoken the language of love together, we would have quoted poetry, Verlaine, Apollonaire, Rimbaud. I wanted to be his dream child, his dream girl. I almost was. I almost thought he was gay. Except there was his bulgy, the smell of it. I could tell he smelled pussy; he just didn't smell mine. I did everything I could. I scented it with lavender. I scented it with clove. I scented it with tea tree, sage, and eucalyptus. I didn't shower for a day, I didn't shower for two, I let it go practically a week. I could tell when I came in 7th he was noticing something; he just didn't notice that he was noticing me. It's me, Mr. Bigdick, it's me that smells! I'm the thing that smells, I'm the thing you're smelling. It's my scented cunt! And then he does like the most fucked up thing in the world. He'd roll out that voluminous U.S. Steel file-drawer of his, I can still

hear the rumbling concatenation of the ball-bearings click-
ing, and pulls out a poem. He'd wrinkle his brow and look
up at the high ceiling as though spotting a minute fly, and say,
*I've got one in the manila!* That's Mr. Bigdick, all right! *I've
got one in the manila*! Whew! That meant he'd got another
poem, or an excerpt, or some literary snicket or passage to
share with me again. And it would of course relate exactly
to what was going on, except it had no relation to it. You
could see his body was reacting; he looked away from me,
he looked elsewhere, he looked askance, he gave a side-long
glance. These were things you taught me, Mr. Bigdick, you
yourself taught me how to see, how to read, and instead of
your long thin fingers on my crooked elbow, which I would
have so much tremulously welcummed, I would have died
over the velvet touch of your didactic brilliance, nay, genius,
touching my arm, I'd be greeted again by the clippety-clop
sound of stainless steel ball-bearings trotting in their tracks,
a hundred little silver balls going around and around. And
then you'd say, listen to this:

> *Music, when soft voices die,*
> *Vibrates in the memory—*
> *Odours, when sweet violets sicken,*
> *Live within the sense they quicken.*
> *Rose leaves, when the rose is dead,*
> *Are heaped for the beloved's bed;*
> *And so thy thoughts, when thou art gone,*
> *Love itself shall slumber on.*

He was so fucking obtuse. He'd smell my love-basket
and not even know it. And then he'd go rip out some poem
to read to me. And of course, what would that be? It'd be

some Shelley no less crying over the death of his beloved. Read, Mr. Bigdick, read! R. E. A. D. What's different about this poem, and a master like Keats, he'd start lecturing me, is that you've got Percy Bysshe looking forward to looking back. Aside from the lugubrious aspect of his being on the edge of his seat to mourn, which is admittedly perverse, it's a straightforward piece, link for link. Everything's normal. Good sounds are recalled. Sweet smells turn sick. Roses symbolize love. When he says, "Love slumbers," it's a little queer, but we swallow it because of the metrical regularity. In other words, we let it go, and it goes down as though it makes sense, which, it really doesn't, unless you suddenly anthropomorphosize love, which you're free to do. Aside from that, it's pretty clockwork. All the more so because it is the sense of smell that is most closely linked with memory, and thus, perfectly fitting for this little piece that considers as a trope the past. Christ! that's what he was like! That's what he would do! And I'm like: You're kidding me, Mr. Bigdick; you've got to be kidding me. You've just smelled my pussy, scattered rose petals all over it, given me a bubble bath, sponged me down, watched me die, thought of me forever, and you now give me some bullshit about tropes? Keats, on the other hand, was concerned with the Eternal Present. And then, goddamnit, he'd do Keats! Keats, he'd say, stood on his tippy-toes and perched a kiss forever there. Can you say, perch a kiss, Bettina? Well, I have. He was one foot next to me. He had Shelley in one hand, and, perching like that shrimp Keats, almost me in the other. A whole year of this. I could have been laid so many times that year, but I kept myself for you. I kept myself for you, Mr. Bigdick. I kept myself pure for you, for you to take me, for me to give myself to you, you insensitive blind mother-fucker. Mr.

Bigdick, you saw nothing. I love this poem, you'd say, and you did, Mr. Bigdick. But don't get me wrong, Keats is the much better poet. Hands down, Bettina. There's no cumpare, really. There's really no cumpare.

# 10

## *Mrs. Bigdick*

Of course I thought he was just maybe a reverse cock-tease. He'd say stuff about Brooke Shield's panties; that's provocative. OK, so it was 7th period, not exactly class time, but in terms of teacher-student relations, it's borderline. He had to have known that. And he'd go from that to erotic love poems. He did cross lines. He had to have known. I never asked him about therapy. I never asked him. He just got to talking in his usual, I shouldn't be telling you about this, but I am, why am I telling you about this kind of way he had and then go on to tell me about, in this case, his therapist, not about therapy itself but where it was. It was like telling me it was going to the gym to him, which to him it was. It's my mental One-a-Day, he said. I don't need therapy, he'd say; nobody actually needs to go to the gym either. We don't need drama, we don't need Shakespeare. What was I supposed to say to that? I agree? But did he need to tell me where his therapist was, I mean physically located? Like a block away from me? I said bye to him one day after swinging by after school to talk. He was talking sort of obliquely about how far he had to drive to work and back, begging the question which I asked and he said Great Barrington.

—Great Barrington, Massachusetts? Wow, that's really far, Mr. Bigdick! Do you do that everyday?

—Sure do. Except when I'm sick in bed with a sack of ice on my head. Home is close enough to smell the blue grass bands of Bennington, and far enough away to forget the unpleasant odor of these run-down hallways. Where do you live?

—Oh, Spruce Street.

—Really, that's where my therapist is.

And that was that. That's how it came out. He was cool, so nonchalant I didn't make anything of it. It was the next day that he said, I didn't think at the time to give you a ride home yesterday; I was going to therapy and could have dropped you off. I guess so, I said, not knowing what to say. Maybe next week, I know where you live, he said. Maybe, I said. I didn't know what to make of it. What was weirder, his telling me about his therapist or offering to drive me home? It never came up again. He never mentioned it again, driving me home.

I blew it. He'd felt me out about driving me in his car, and I blew it! How's therapy, I got up the courage to say to him once. Therapeutic, he said. I once had a girlfriend whose brother asked their father, when I was over at their house, a doctor who sang in Italian around the house, what acrimonious meant. Without looking up from his newspaper he said, acrid. And that, Bettina, is how I find therapy. I wasn't trying to pry, Mr. Bigdick, I was only asking. I was actually trying to get up the gumption really to ask him to drive me home. But I blew that too. It was Tuesday, and that was the day he did it, went to therapy. And I was trying to ask him to drive me home on his way to therapy. He was probably pissed from the first time that I didn't go with him, which is why he brought up the acrimonious thing, trying to make me jealous. But I'm not that way anyway. I was really mad at myself, not him. He had every right not to go with me. What was I saying? Oh, my God, I was going mad. I needed therapy. What about a therapist for me, Mr. Bigdick? He just smiled a big big smile. I am your therapist, Bettina. I am your therapist. You don't need another. I'm the only one you'll ever need. For the rest of your life. He was a little spooky at times. I wasn't always quite sure what he was saying. You could take him so many ways. Well, OK, then, I said, you can be it. See you tomorrow, then. See you tomorrow, Bettina. Hope your therapy goes well or whatever you're supposed to say about therapy.

If he was my therapist, oh my God was I in for it.

I was still talking to Xsu-Xsu then. About this sort of. Before she went off the face of the planet. She was my best friend until she went to Harvard. She talked about your own personal space, and my cumfort zone, and monitoring myself. Like what, I'm a video camera? I'm grateful that she listened, but that's about it. I wasn't about to tell her though that I was the one trying to get Mr. Bigdick to fuck me, not the other way around. But she was like: Why would Mr. Bigdick want to do anything with you? She didn't mean it as an insult. She meant it literally, just like she meant everything literally. Doesn't he have a wife? By that she meant, should he be married, why would he be involved with another female? To her it was like, if you already know you're going to go over the George Washington Bridge into Manhattan, why is it important to know what the traffic is like at the Holland Tunnel? If she only knew about his wife: The Invalid. Mr. Bigdick like never mentioned her. But when he did it was just that: The Invalid. I felt bad for him, having to live with a wife like that. He didn't say it mean like he hated her or that they hated each other. Some kids said they knew about her, that it was a car accident or something. It was sad for him. I mean, here he was, definitely still even with college the most intelligent person I've ever met with in my life with an invalid for a wife. Life just isn't fair, is it? And it isn't fair to me. Why would he not want me if he had an invalid for a wife? I wasn't going to ruin anything between them. It's not like I wanted to marry him myself. I just wanted to fuck him, to get him to do me, to be the first one, to be able to look back some day and say, the first guy I ever did was Mr. Bigdick, my AP English teacher. Can you believe I once thought he was really smart? I'm just kidding about that. No, really. But it didn't work out that way. I did a lot of other guys, and most of the time, when they were old and creepy, I was thinking of him.

My Mr. Bigdick. My Mr. Bigdick he wasn't afraid. He wasn't afraid of anything. My Mr. Bigdick wandered down the boulevardes of Paris with me, we strolled down *les jardins*, past the Tuileries, him and me. It sounds better that way. Instead of he and I. That doesn't work. He and I wandered down past the Tuileries with a slice of brie. Oh, him and me. He was afraid to sniff the little vapors of my camembert, the sweet eau de cologne of my berth, and that's with an *e*, not an *i* of course. Mr. Bigdick he taught me to write. Most people when they write, don't hear anything. How can people be so sensitive as to hear one picayune mosquito in a circus tent and not the nasal sound of their own inane vowels? Just listen to it Bettina, the mid-Atlantic homogeneity: Mary, marry, merry. Say them, he said. And I did. OK, you'll pass. I passed! I was past more than just the gates of St. Michael. I met his didactic approval! I passed his scholastic standards. I greeted his pedagogical predictions. I could feel my Mr. Bigdick smelling my cheese. To be called a writer, to be a writer, that was the zenith of my happiness. My Mr. Bigdick looked over my proofs, when he was finished with his own daily labors of the classroom of course, and edited my work. I saw him with the yellow stub of a number 2 pencil in one hand and the accompanying magnifying glass to the two-volume set of the glorious O.E.D. in the other. The O.E.D., that venerable sewer, he called it, into which has settled the precipitate of Norman time. My Mr. Bigdick went over my work as a writer. And my work was all about him. What a genius he was. I could never pay him back, any more than the bean seeds the summer rain for sprouting. He was my mentor, my guide. My Mr. Bigdick was my spiritual father. And that made it OK to fuck him. Which I was determined to do. No matter what. Even if I didn't write a word under his nose, I would fuck him. I was going to fuck my English teacher, Mr. Bigdick. No matter what. Even if I ended up with a 2 on my AP exam, which I didn't, I got a 5, I was going to fuck him. That was the chapter in my book I was going to write. And I was going to make him help me do it. But my Mr. Bigdick never came over. He just went to therapy. He took his One-a-Day for mental health, and I peddled my blue bike home alone without him and jerked off.

I almost never barely got personal with him. One time I asked about his wife straight up. We were just talking 7th and I was wearing a denim skirt that showed me having a lot wider hips than I actually do but I like to wear it because it feels cumfortable; I don't, like a lot of things, care what other people think, and I said to him actually, like we'd been talking about it, "like your wife," and like that he started talking. He looked down past his lap at the ochre floor, like a rower about to row, that simile sucks I know, and looked up and started to talk. Beth. Kleigmann. Jew. The Invalid. What, I said? My wife, Beth Kleigmann is an invalid Jew. Then, I already felt bad. I'd known about her already from Xsu-Xsu. All the kids knew the story. We didn't have the same story of course. But we all knew the story. One version of it was Mr. Bigdick and his wife were trashed after New Year's, and they got hit by another car coming back home. Somewhere in Maine. Mr. Bigdick was driving. She got paralyzed. Another version was his wife was actually in Hazlewood, New York and got it turning left on Route 11. A mail truck slammed into her from behind. We saw it as kind of a joke of course, being hit by a mail truck, because there aren't jokes of course about anybody being hit by a mail truck. So, it's like ironic. It's not like being hit by a Mack truck is the point. It would be like cracking your head open falling off a scooter. Nobody does, so it's embarrassing when it happens. Another version is she was just backed into at a mall somewhere. Whatever it was, they all were in cars, and that's how Mrs. Bigdick got paralyzed. The worst part was now I had to listen to it first-hand like I'd never heard anything about it before. I felt bad because it was personal. And I felt bad because I couldn't stop him now that I'd started him. I couldn't say, wait, wait, wait, Mr. Bigdick, I know about her, I'm sorry I asked, let's just skip it. I'm sorry it ever happened, I mean, about your wife. I really felt bad for him. It was a mistake that I couldn't stop. I did try though. Really, I said, she's Jewish? Yes, and an invalid. I don't know why I'm telling you these things, Bettina, I really shouldn't, but I am telling you these things, I always do. You don't have to, Mr. Bigdick. This of course was our standard 7th period preamble to anything interesting. Denial.

Denial. Revelation. It always worked like that. I didn't know she was Jewish, I lied. Yes, she's Jewish. But you'd never know it, not just by looking at her. Do you know the picture *Christina's World* by Wyeth? I think so, I lied again. And he opened up his closet door with his skeleton key, the kind pirates have to open treasure chests, and on the back of it was a picture of a big field and a barn in the background. In front, there was a woman in the wheat. You can't see her face. This picture, I keep it here to remind me of her. Of your wife, is that her name? No, Beth. Not Christina? No, Beth. She looks very pretty, Mr. Bigdick, except you can't see her face. She is. What's she doing in the middle of the field? Well, we're all grown up here, at least one of us is, he said: She was dumped off her wheelchair. I was suddenly very confused. Mr. Bigdick could be like that. He'd be very sincere, very solemn, and then the next thing that came out of his mouth was just so wrong. You couldn't really tell really if he was joking or not. I'm sorry to hear that, I said. You weren't the driver, Bettina. Were you? Now I was fishing. And I was more curious, honestly, than guilty. I already had felt bad enough about bringing it up, but now that he was talking about it, I figured I'd find out from the horse's mouth what the real story was. Are you saying your Jewish wife is in a wheelchair, Mr. Bigdick? My wife, I just call her The Invalid; not to her face; to her face I call her Beth because that's her name: Beth. But when I'm talking about her, I call her The Invalid, because, well, she is. My wife, you may, I'm guessing, have heard some stories, people do make them up, we are story-makers all of us. Lee Harvey Oswald. John Wilkes Booth. Squeaky Fromme. Valerie Solanus. People murder people and we make up stories about them. They're never the truth. They're stories. Remember that, Bettina. Truth is like the moment a story's done, you close your eyes; and for a second there, listen. Then it's gone. That's truth. Anyway, one late afternoon I was peeling an orange. This is what I remember most about it. The orange peel in the kitchen sink. And a trooper pulls into my driveway real slow. There was just one, I could see that out through the kitchen window through the squad car's glass that it was tinted and that there was only one, which struck me odd. I dropped the paring knife. No, yes, I don't remember if I was peeling the orange with a knife or not. Why would I peel an orange with a knife, Bettina? Do you peel oranges with a knife? I don't know, Mr. Bigdick; I guess I've never peeled one. Really? I don't know. I knew something was wrong. He came to the door and told me the news. She'd been hit head-on. I suppose like most marriages it probably would have ended in divorce after three or four more years with an equitable distribution of assets. The impact was so great there wasn't really any person to identify. The contents of her purse: Address book, lipsticks, a bit of mirror, broken comb, teeth, tampon fluff, the usual paraphernalia were smashed and scattered all over the road. It was a good car, a BMW. I'm sorry, Mr. Bigdick, I'm sorry, I'm really sorry I ever brought it up. It was, he said, a total waste of a new car. I asked him if there was anything I could do. His eyes were like saucers. My Mr. Bigdick looked so old and sad. It was also disgusting that I ever wanted to fuck him now that I looked at it. He was like my father. And that's really gross. She was like the blond Christina, only she was Jewish, Bettina. She's still alive, isn't she? Alive, and, he said, I won't say it. You can say it, Mr. Bigdick. You can say it, I said. And kicking. I keep this poster tacked to the back of my closest to remind myself that she isn't a Christian cripple in the field; she's a

Jew. She's my wife. She's a total invalid. That's why I call her that. Doesn't Kliegmann make it sort of obvious, though, that she's a Jew, I asked? It could be German, he said. It's got two n's. Oh, I said. I see. I lied a third time. I really didn't.

That was about the only time I really got personal with him. You can see why.

He was a weirdo *par excellence*. That's why he's so great. Was, anyway. I mean who else would impersonate a rapist? Who else would spit real red blood stuff into a white hand-kerchief whisked from his pocket and cumpose out loud *Ode to a Nightingale*, not the whole thing, just the *Was it a vision, or a waking dream* part? Who else brings in whole hacked up garlic bulbs and puts them over his eyes for gouged out sockets at the end of *Oedipus*? Who else would play Grendel in John Gardner's book throwing apples at Unferth and actually throw apples at us actually breaking a window? The best was when Mr. Bigdick played Lucky and I played Pozzo in *Waiting for Godot*. He'd brought in a real noose, cumplete with thirteen hitches, which he placed over his own neck. When I pulled it, which my character is sup-posed to, I could see he meant for me to really pull on it. So, I did. He was like clawing at the rope around his neck which was really tight because I was really pulling. But I didn't let go. Nope. I kept it taut. Just the way he was telling me to with his telling eyes. He was like a Houdini Mr. Bigdick wanting me to torture him with something he couldn't actu-ally escape out of. That was the act. When Lucky explodes into his rant that goes on for four or five pages without a break, we thought he was going to really explode and have a stroke. His face was devil-red and the veins on his forehead and his neck bulged out like a heart attack. It was gross to look at, all that pumping blood. People in the hallway looked through the little square glass window in the middle of the door at all the noise inside to see what was going on and just left because you could see they were afraid of what was happening. They just left. The rope was burning around Mr. Bigdick's neck; I kept it tight, and he just kept screaming and screaming out Lucky's lines for about fifteen minutes straight uninterrupted until they were done. He was crazy. And then he'd stop, catch his breath like an Olympic runner and bring up very calmly the irony of the master/servant relationship with one smooth hand, and dish out a packet of Nietzsche about slave morality for us to read with his slender-fingered other. He was great. Mr. Bigdick, if it's possible to be so, he was really a conscious madman. He had no system, but he was perfectly organized. Perfectly.

How did I appreciate Mr. Bigdick? Let me count my ways. First of all he had a big dick. Like I described. Second, he knew a lot. And, I also liked his fingers, the way they moved. I'd think about those fingers moving all over around my body. Like spiders, the way they investigate. I had a lot of guys, just last year, and they investigated me, but not the way Mr. Bigdick would. He'd take his time. He'd rub my breast, he'd rub my stomach, he'd rub my pussy, he'd rub my ass, he'd rub my legs. He'd massage me all over. He'd massage my temples with his pointer fingers and talk perhaps slowly about the solar plexus. He'd rub my temples and talk about college, when he was there, the things he did. He'd talk about love and who I'd known and wouldn't be jealous. He'd accept me for who I am. He'd crack my legs open and stick in his tongue. He'd move it round and round like he was twirling a mini beach-ball, like the multi-colored spinning ones on Macs spinning and spinning and spinning in OS X. He'd twirl me and twirl me on his tongue like a little mini beachball like that and I'd go round, I'd go round and I'd be his girl. I'd be his hump. I'd be his cunt. I'd be his lay. I'd be his dirty flaxen-haired fuck. I'd be his little cum-buddy. I'd let it in, the cum, since I'd already had my shot anyway, and it wouldn't matter. Then I'd ooze around his creative genius juice inside me. Then I'd play a rôle reversal where I'd be the classroom. I'd be the teacher and say: Sit Down, Enright! Sit Down! And he would. Then I'd say: Now today, Enright, quote me a poem! And he would. Then I'd say: Quote me some Emily Dickinson! And he would. Quote me some Robert Frost! And he would. Quote me some Sexton, Plath, and some John Berryman! And he would. He would do it all, humping and bumping me, squirts of verses and cum pouring out of him. He'd be the total poetry-quoting squirt-dog of my affection. My Enright Bigdick. I really had a thing for him. But I don't think the shit ever really had it for me. I don't think he cared a shit about me. He really didn't.

# 11

## *France (junior year abroad)*

When I went away that year to France my junior year I wrote him so many times. I wrote him from the Musée d'Orsay, the one where they keep all the Fauves, all the rejects from the 1800's that got really famous later. I wrote to tell him how all the colors of that totally Tahitian madman Gauguin were there all creamy and bright, just like he said. *Oh, oui, c'est vrai Monsieur Bigdick, l'orange il n'est pas la même orange dans une autre langue.* Yes, Mr. Bigdick, it pretty much goes, the color orange is not the same orange in another language. I wanted to tell him, I wanted to exclaim, and I did! All the things he told were true and more, even better, about France than I had ever imagined possible. Just as I was getting it up the ass by an Arab, a real Tunisian, I heard Mr. Bigdick. When I was in Monastir, and this is a tourist city for the French and German, I swam off one afternoon past the sandstone cliffs off of which we would dive into the Mediterranean blue blue water, to an island covered with abandoned industrial machinery. It was all heavy and rusted. I had swum, you can say *swam* or *swum*, and I tend to vacillate depending on whatever Hungarian back-vowel I've got spinning in my head comes down the back of my throat between the two; I'd swim swam swum off to this abandoned island looking for Roman grottos with a local sinewy and dark and pimply boy who told me he knew where they were. And just as he was pointing down into a dark subterranean hole, he put his dark mulatto finger up to his lips and said, *Juste un peu, s'il te plaît?* Touching his lips again, he repeated to me, *Juste un peu?* And just as I felt Latiffe my Tunisian stallion exploding his Arabic cum up my ass, I heard and saw Mr. Bigdick's story galloping between my ears, telling me the end of his Tunisian tale. *Please, just a little bit?* I just looked at him, Bettina, and began walking away. I couldn't run because the ground was sharp, volcanic. I didn't turn back and when I reached the edge of the island dove softly into the blue warm water and swam calmly to shore. Wow! Whew! Even in Paris, Mr. Bigdick was right there up my ass even when Latiffe was, even when the salt tears of laughter pain and sorrow were coming out of my eyes. You were there Mr. Bigdick. I felt you. Whether they were principal parts, Paris pictures, the colorful pipes of Pompidou pigments, or purulent Arabs popping up my poop shoot, when Latiffe came like a tidal wave of Saharan sand up my ass, I felt you all the time, Mr. Bigdick. Paris was just incredible, I wrote him. How often I think of you Mr. Bigdick, I wrote. And I wrote to him about all my cultural experiences that really didn't mean shit to me. I wrote to him about all the French authors I read, all the French anecdotal experiences I was having in the fabled City of Light; I wrote to him about French solitude and self. Gosh, I probably bored him to death with all the incredible French things I was seeing and eating and hearing. But do you think Mr. Bigdick ever really guessed what I was really thinking about, about him doing me up the ass on the second floor of a creaky French hotel on all fours like a farm animal? I doubt it. I really doubt it.

Maybe not. I got this one letter from him. It was incredible. I threw it out. It was stupid of me. I was mad. The best part of it was the leaves. He sent me Autumn. He filled an envelope with yellow leaves. They were all maple. From his backyard. I remember opening the envelope. It came like a pillow. And boom. The smell of Fall was in my face. I whipped off my panties. I lit pachouli. I clubbed myself to oblivion chanting as the smoke filled my eyes, Bigdick, Bigdick, Bigdick! A lot of the leaves got pretty torn up on my bed under my ass from moving around so much. I kept one, just one, on my windowsill for months while I was away and admired its blackened crumpling silhouette against the setting sun at vespers. But that was it. That was the last of his romantic overtures. Not that I expected him to send me snowflakes for Winter. But I felt so embarrassed that I'd jerked off to that jerk that I threw the whole pack of leaves and the note inside away. Except the one on the sill. I kept that for posterity.

I probably should have said something about how I really felt. I mean, if he'd have made like a pass at me and I'd gone to the Board or the principal or my parents, even though he was revered, that would have been the end of Mr. Bigdick at HHS. It'd happened already to one teacher, and what he did was mild cumpared to what I had in mind. The band teacher, Mr. Ollo, was caught with just shitloads and shitloads of naked little girls in his hard drive. One day he was waving a baton to some crappy Steven Sondheim tune, and the next his wrists are wrapped in these Glad®-bag kind of disposable-looking cinch-cuffs they've got these days. I saw him in the paper with his chin tucked down like one of those second pin Italian godfather types. It's like they're penitent or praying or something. But they're not. They're just pathetic. That was what Mr. Ollo looked like. I was in marching band with him for three years before it happened. What a loser. I mean they say the girls were from Belgium and Spain and I think France even, Europeans mostly, and they were all about nine or eight. I can't even understand who'd want that. I wouldn't. I wanted Mr. Bigdick. I would never have gotten him in any trouble. Never. Mr. Ollo, he just looked at sick pictures and one day asked a girl, who by the way was a real whore already, out to coffee across the street. Nothing more than that. She took it the wrong way, and the next day they SWAT-teamed his house with like riot gear and everything and left with him in those garbage bag closer handcuffs and his cumputer. I heard that his screen-saver was this like six year old giving head to like a seventy year old man. But that's probably a lie. Kids always do. I know. I've done plenty of it myself. So, basically, he got snagged because he sort of hit on the wrong girl, if going out for coffee is even considered that, and it led to just the wrong thing for him. It's probably for the best, though. It's just sort of creepy having a guy like that who can even think those things being your music teacher or any other. Not that I'm into Thought Police. I don't believe in Big Brothering people or fingerprinting, but it's nice to know that your music teacher just wants you to learn a part for high voice or something, and isn't like out trying to smell the air outside your bedroom at 3 A.M. , three o'clock in the morning through a window. Given what had happened to Mr. Ollo just the year before, I guess Mr. Bigdick just wanted to play it safe. I really should have been up front. I really should have told him what I thought. I really should have told him how

I felt. I should have said: Mr. Bigdick, you've got a lot more experience in life than me at this point, but I think you're a totally amazing person. I should have said: Mr. Bigdick, next to my parents there's no one in the world who's made a greater impact on me and had more influence than you. I should have said: Mr. Bigdick, I've been really admiring you basically since the day we met between my junior and senior year. I should have said: Mr. Bigdick, I hope you remember that day you met me and Xsu-Xsu, and told me, us, I should say, to take Calculus instead of AP English. I should have said: Because of you, I wanted to major in English in college. I should have said: Mr. Bigdick, I am truly very sorry that I took up so much of your 7th periods. I should have said: Mr. Bigdick, I ought to have told you that neither my mother or father, 9 to 5ers, were home for two hours past school, and you could have come over to my house. I should have said: Mr. Bigdick, our secret would have been as safe as a baby in its mother's crib. I should have said: I would never have asked of you more than you could give. I should have said: Mr. Bigdick, I will never interfere with or make demands upon you that would compromise your home life. I should have said: Mr. Bigdick, people will never understand the connection between us, so I will never say a thing. I should have said: Mr. Bigdick, I want to feel your huge big dick inside me. I should have said: Mr. Bigdick, I want to feel you slam me up against the wall. I should have said: Mr. Bigdick, I want to feel you hump me. I should have said: Mr. Bigdick, I trust and respect whatever your decision is. I should have said: Whatever happens to us, our trust will be eternal. I should have said: Mr. Bigdick, as long as you will have me, I will be yours. I should have said: Mr. Bigdick, my affection for you is truly at your disposal. I should have said: Mr.

Bigdick, if you wish to here and now discard my affection for you, I will understand. I should have said: Mr. Bigdick, no matter what happens between us, I will always remember you. I should have said a lot of things that I didn't. Instead, I told him all the most typical things the most typical high school girl will tell a teacher. It's all my fault. I gave him no impression that I wanted his big dick. It was all my fault. I probably could have landed him like a big fish, but I never cast the line. I never cast the line. I truly regret it.

What a motherfucker he was though. I mean it. He had no right to go on letting me listen to him drone on and on and on all those 7th periods and then all of a sudden one day out of the blue tell me to get lost. Very pedagogical it was of him. He did it very properly of course. He did basically everything very properly. It was in him to do everything properly. He parsed poetry properly. He cited works properly. He dressed pretty properly. He spoke properly. When he got excited, he got excited properly. When he was passionate, he was properly so. He was indeed very passionate, but kept really his distance the way a lion tamer knows just how close he can get to his giant cats. What, was I going to maul him? Were we going to maul him like lions to pieces? I don't think so. I was going to love him. That's what he was afraid of I think. I hate Mr. Bigdick for that. He's the one who wouldn't even let me get close. It was he or him I really don't give a fuck now him or he, who cares, he made and kept that distance between us. It was masochistic. It was mean. It was just plain mean to make me like him so much and not let me get any closer to him than the length of a closed file cabinet. Physically, that's how he was. I always felt like that between us, like there was a file cabinet. How could you lead a girl on like that, Mr. Bigdick, and then not respond to her? It's so capricious. It's so whimsical. That's what I should have asked him. When I wrote those myriad letters from France to Mr. Bigdick, that's what I should have said. Why are you so mean? Instead, I talked about everything else that was just so blasé and unimportant. If he ever had had any interest in fucking me, I'm sure he lost it then. Everything's my fault. I blew it.

The picture of me and Mr. Bigdick I had was idyllic. It was like the one he had on the back of his door but different. The back door of his closet was the secret to everything about him. The one, solitary picture of *Christina's World* told me much. It told me too much perhaps. It told me for sure that for all his invective, and, boy did I ever hear it 7th period, I think he really loved America. It told me that for all his words to the contrary, Mr. Bigdick did somewhere really and truly admire American art. He had a soft spot for it. Oh, he'd talk the opposite. *You can replace Susan Sontag's the white race is the cancer of human history*, he said, *with "Americans" for "white race." That, when Susan Sontag spoke, is what she really means. It wasn't*, he said, *the white race itself that blew apart the forests of Vietnam, it was the Americans*. Well and good, Mr. Bigdick. Well and good. But there you had it, just a notch or two up from Norman Rockwell, pinned up there against his pine closet door: *Christina's World*; it's right up there with *Whistler's Mother* as one of two best-loved clichés of American Art. Back then, I didn't know about it then back then. Back then, I didn't know shit about art. Back then, I was like a virgin. And I was, too. I was his untouched Christina. I rhymed with it, I rhymed with it, Mr. Bigdick. I rhymed. Bettina with

Christina. It was so obvious. But he didn't even hear it. In the picture I tack to his wall, I'm not even in it. Take Christina out. Picture a wheatfield, Mr. Bigdick. Picture big, old American barns in the background. Make the wheat windswept and golden-yellow. The wind has been blowing across here since before the buffalo. Since before the Indians. It's just grass. Not even wheat. It's just the plains of America and grass has been blown here by the wind forever. Since before people were. White people. Or Indians. And then, centuries and centuries later there's a farmhouse and a barn built. Then it's you and me. Birds are flying in it. You and I are in the barn alone. That's why you can't see us in my picture. We're in love in the barn.

Mr. Bigdick, you could have had me in your world. Not just a cripple you had for a wife. The wind could have blown all day through wheat, and I would have been standing there, not just waiting and waiting and waiting. I would have been running to you Mr. Bigdick. *Bettina's World* is a picture just of a barns and wheatfields. I've run off the canvas into the barn. You can't see us because we're in there making love. We've left the doors open a little bit to let in enough light to see around. There's an old milk pail I've kicked over when we first got in to be funny, and there's an old rusty pitchfork nobody's used in decades stuck in a pile of dried up manure that doesn't even smell anymore it's so rock-hard, and there's you standing over me. You hold me passionately down in the barn straw and do it to me with real oomph. Up in the rafters the barn swallows flutter. Up in the rafters the mice scutter. Up in the rafters my burly-armed farmer, Mr. Bigdick.

Pondering this dream many a night I one day realized many other things about it. The first thing is what is

Christina doing out there in Wyeth's picture? Sure, it looks beautiful, and you're right, Mr. Bigdick, Americans really are dumb. You put a woman sideways with her hips jutting up on the side in a pink dress in a country setting and it looks so beautiful. Wyeth's cruelty is all over the place, you said: Look at the automobile tracks; they're not even close to her. They mock her open captivity. The whole picture, you claimed, was about control and captivity, trapping like a bunny rabbit in a snare the female form within the handiwork of the rectangle picture frame which captures everything in it for the male eye to freely ogle over. Bravo, Mr. Bigdick, bravo! Not only with impunity, no, it rewards our doing so, giving these rapscallion purveyors the clubbish sense of being cultured. Bravo, again! But it was on your door, your coat closet door, Mr. Bigdick; what you so ironically labeled your office door: A bunch of shelves filled with high school teacher texts, mementos from students forgotten, stacks of leftover Styrofoam® cups, and whatever other detritus an English teacher, you said yourself, piles up after decades of stagnation, and worst of all, you said, social abandonment. It then swept across me. The picture of *Christina's World* there didn't really have to do anything with remembering your wife like you told me it did. That was a lie, I'm afraid, Mr. Bigdick. I'm sorry about her, I really am. It was all about you. You were stranded. You were marooned. You were crippled. There at Harrisford High. You were The Invalid. You called your wife that, it was weird, and then I got what it was about. You've been really talking about yourself the whole time, Mr. Bigdick. You can't even see that it's you who's in that American of American pictures, stuck there, crippled there, alone there, out there alone in the windswept mid-western grass of America. You were abandoned. You were trapped. I said in my heart that I was going to rescue you.

I was walking along the Seine in Paris one evening with an English boy who'd just done me a minute ago; it was kinda gross, and he told me this story. In England, he said, it's fairly common to throw oneself into the Thames. When the bodies are recovered, there are two main differences. There are those whose fingers are puckered and soft, and there are those whose fingertips, he told me, are raked to the bone. The Thames, he said, was buttressed by concrete walls, you see. Those whose fingers were puckered and soft, died for death. Those whose fingers were raked, died for life. These are the sorts of suicides London has, he said. Those who die for death, and those who die for life. And it was then at that very precise moment, it was at the very moment that I felt a small portion of his English cum trickle down that I thought precisely of you, Mr. Bigdick. I was going to save you from the soft-fingered suicide, alone at Harrisford High. You were so sad, Mr. Bigdick. I was going to save you. You were in the field alone. I saw it. I saw it on your back door. And even if I had to heap you up in a wheelbarrow, I was going to take you into that barn and save you. I was going to bring you back to life. If it was the last thing I did. I swore it to myself. I am going to do Mr. Bigdick, if it's the last thing.

I should have known I was kidding myself. All those letters I sent, they didn't mean shit, not a thing. Not racy enough? Not enough pith? Not enough stuff? How was I, just a girl in France, going to really save the guy with some fancy pink French stationary? I was really kidding myself. It was like he said about listening to foreigners speak your language: You had to have the willingness and ability to understand what somebody else speaking your language was saying to understand it. And he obviously didn't want to understand me. I'm speaking the language of love to him. The French stamps alone should have done it. But did he get it? Of course not. I never figured he was really so obtuse really. Able? Well, he wasn't really that old. A guy with a cock the size Mr. Bigdick's smelled in Banana Republic™ khakis, he should have been able to get it up big time. Big time. Right. I just don't think he was willing anymore. Somebody told me about Buddhism and told me that when the student is ready the teacher will appear. Hello, Mr. Bigdick? I was ready, and you were the teacher. But did you appear? Nope, you just stayed in your schoolroom grading papers and getting old by yourself there. I didn't abandon you Mr. Bigdick. You abandoned yourself. And then you abandoned me. That's the part that hurt. It just wasn't fair. It just didn't feel fair anymore.

I couldn't really cumpletely blame him though. There was the story about Mr. Boston, remember? And the way things are now about relationships in the classroom, girls wanting to get back at a teacher can just say *his eyes fell on one of my breasts and stayed there on it and made me feel uncumfortable*, and a teacher is basically gone. I couldn't entirely blame him. But that was like three years back, so what was he hanging onto? The times they are a-changin', Mr. Bigdick. Even I know who Bob Dylan was and what he means. Don't you? But you go on and on with the *Kreutzer Sonata*, and Tolstoy, and then The Emerson String Quartet's playing Beethoven's opus 59, #2, and I'm supposed to be more impressed with them than Dylan? I like Beethoven, don't get me wrong, I'm hardly a philistine. I'm hip. I've got like a 80 gig iPod. But sex is sex. Time is time. And years are years. Three big ones had gone by. He'd missed digging out my little root cellar in high school. And like a hundred thirty-seven truffles dug up in me the last I counted, there's still a lot more pig-rootin' in me to be done. I hate to sound even cornier than I am, but you can lead a big dick to water, but you can't make it drink. Nope. He just wasn't willing.

# 12

## The WTC

What stops a guy from wanting to be saved? What stops a guy from wanting to fuck me? My grades are good, my tits look pretty hot in a tank top, and I speak two languages. That's not all of course. There's more, but a guy twice my age who doesn't want to fuck me's got a problem. Guys Mr. Bigdick's age would pay big time, as it were, just to do me just once or twice. I know. They have. Not like prostitution really. Just fancy dinners. Five star restaurants. And I do them. I mean I like them, too. I just don't pay for the dinners. I'm too young to. I don't have a salary. I'm just a student. That's the only reason. And it's fun. It's fun to be taken out, wined and dined, and to later suck on some old nice guy's cock. They really are grateful, not like young guys, as I've said before. So, if Mr. Bigdick didn't want me, it was his problem.

It was my problem though. I have to admit it too. I hate it too. When a guy like Mr. Bigdick, totally brilliant, doesn't want you, it's hard not to feel it as a negative self-reflection. I hate thinking about it, but I do. I really think the reason I fucked so many old guys, and by old I mean older than twenty years older than myself, is because of him. I have to admit, too, that it was kind of unfair to them. That I was taking advantage of them. But who were they anyway, fucking a girl who was easily their daughters' own age? It's still pretty gross if you ask me, but I did it; so, who cares? I mean what's age anyway? Numbers are just years, something like that, aren't they? I thought if I fucked enough guys older than myself, I'd find the right one. But I never do. They were always cumparisons, although they never knew it. That's the unfair part. But I was really trying to forget you, Mr. Bigdick, once and for all. I just couldn't. In fact, the more old guys I fucked, the more I thought of you. My feelings for you became like a rose tattoo tattooed on the inside of my heart. I think part of the reason he rejected me is I was just young. Is that possible? Sometimes it got all very confusing and I just found myself in Paris alone writing poems and crying about it. I know it sounds pretty pathetic, but that's how it was really. The city of love for me was more like a city of despair, a feeling I'd never felt in my life before. Never. I'm normally a very happy person. I always am really. But Paris made me really moody. I just missed Mr. Bigdick and wanted to tell him in person. But after he sent me the autumn package of leaves from the Berkshire Mountains, that was it. No more. Nothing. I sent him more and more French letters, and he didn't answer a one of them. Not a one. I was really sad about it. But I got over it too. Besides Mr. Bigdick, Paris was really great. I did more guys there than any one other place there is. Say what you want, even in the middle of despair, Paris is still the city of love. And everything they say about French men, it's really true. They are what you always dream they are. So much of what I dreamed and hoped for in life has come true. I need hardly to mention, except for Mr. Bigdick. He was like a bee in my bonnet in a way, even though I know that that's not really the right expression for it. That's sort of what it felt like though. An invisible bee always there buzzing around in my bonnet, telling me with its silent buzzing buzz that he was always there. It got to be really annoying at times, but I just couldn't help it. He was such a truly amazing man. Not like he's dead now or anything. How lucky I was to have had him as my teacher, and to have known him personally. Not every girl can count herself so lucky. I'm glad I still can. I really am.

When the airplanes rode into the towers I decided to make one last try to win Mr. Bigdick's heart. A heart is made of stone. A heart is made of ice. A heart is made of many things. And like Blake himself said, "Cruelty has a human heart." And that's what the problem with Mr. Bigdick's was. He just wasn't being kind to his heart. I was going to break through that. If the terrorists were going to fly their engines into the WTC, I was going to burst through the concrete walls of Mr. Bigdick's isolation. He just needed a place to put himself. He needed to learn that he didn't always have to be so professional, that he could be really personal. He needed to understand that he could call me up and put his long slender dick in me. So, I called him up, like I said a lot earlier.

The way it was supposed to be, because I just left him a message, like I said earlier, was that he'd call me back. That much he did. The way it was supposed to be, he told me how much he thought about me when I was away. The way it was supposed to be, he asked me how France was. The way it was supposed to be, he apologized for not having written me. The way it was supposed to be, I forgave him and said it was OK. The way it was supposed to be, he said that I was back and that that's what mattered. The way it was supposed to be, I said I agreed and that I missed him so much too. The way it was supposed to be, we made plans to meet together somewhere, like the Cloister Café on 9th Street, I love that place, ASAP. I love to say that: ASAP. The way it was supposed to be, that's what happened, and we did. The way it was supposed to be, when we met and I had an espresso and he had one, too, he professed not only that he had missed me terribly, but that he cared for me. The way it was supposed to be, I said I did, too. The way it was supposed to be, he confessed his love for me. The way it was supposed to be, I did, too. That's the way it's supposed to be, but did it happen? No, not even close.

Christina!

Very funny, Mr. Bigdick.

So, what's this about the KFC?

The WTC, it's the WTC, you know, the World Trade Center.

So, someone's slamming into the old bucket of chicken? Pennies everywhere?

It's not funny. This just happened.

What just happened, Bettina? Tell me.

I just got out of the shower. I'm standing here with next to nothing on, and I hear this huge whirring sound.

Whirring?

You know, like in an airport. That noise.

A huge *roaring* sound . . .

And it's right over my head. And then, with a towel wrapped around my wet hair, tied up because it's so long now, I watch a huge jet plane airliner lumber into the side of the WTC.

With a towel on, wrapped around your head. And that's it? You're wearing nothing else?

Like what do you mean?

Like maybe clothes, like maybe you're dressed?

No, I just stepped out of the shower, and the towel's the only thing I've got on.

Just around your head?

Yes.

I see. Half-sexy. Half-dressed. Which half is which?

And I'm calling, or I was, just to see if you're OK.

I'm a hundred thirty miles away, north, but I'm fine. I haven't exactly stepped out of the shower with you. You're the one closer to the big chicken bucket.

Mr. Bigdick, really. There's billowing smoke rolling like thunder—

Yuck! Strike that.

—billowing smoke pouring out—

That works.

—from downtown. I saw it fly straight into it.

It? Feed me "it." What's the antecedent, Bettina? Besides, you haven't even said a word about France. Don't be troubled by the women in France; she told him the time when he asked her to dance.

An airliner flew into the side of the WTC.

Really? You're not joking?

Really.

I thought this was ex-student harasses former AP English teacher day, but I guess at 10:17 A.M., we're talking about a real McCoy. Live wire central. 36-piece capitalistic special: Arms, legs, thighs, breasts, white and dark meat. Tell you what. Fuck the bucket. Let's make it All-you-can-eat. On me, of course. Why not? A family affair. National tragedy sort of thing. Pearl Harbor re-dux. Well, Bettina, I've been looking for the perfect excuse for you to come back up here myself and wrinkle the sheets with me, the old crippled missus notwithstanding, and I think you've got it. Hit the bull in the eye sort of thing. Next to a tidal wave sweeping over the western coast of Asia killing three hundred thousand gleefully garbed brown-skinned creatures living the balmy life of third-world deprivation and innocence, and the ensuing global mourning over such calamitous event, I can't think of an incident more conducive to my transgressing the boundaries of avuncular soothing. So, come right on up, Bettina. Come right on up. I'll save you a drumstick, cole slaw, and a pickle.

That bastard, he didn't take me seriously. He really didn't. It wasn't like that. Not *verbatim*. But it just as well could have been. I called him because I was worried. And he was so sarcastic. I couldn't take it. He just made fun of me. I never should have called. It was a mistake. He mocked me for calling him. He mocked me for caring about him. That's all it was. And he made fun of it.

That was the thing, though, you just couldn't tell. Was he harassing you or not? I mean harassing like being mean to, not like wanting to do something. That's different. That's what I wanted. But to be mean to be mean to me, I didn't want that. Certainly not. And it felt like he was just out there to make fun of my kindness. I mean, sure, maybe it is kinda lame to call a teacher up that you've had to see how they are after something like the WTC when you're really just using something bad happening as an excuse to get to know them more, I can see that much, it's obvious, but that doesn't invite them to be so sarcastic either. The WTC was serious, it still is, and he just took it like I'd said a batch of papier mâché mix got hard too fast and to pour some fresh water in and mix another. It was like, whoops, no big deal. He was so flip, I couldn't not help feeling what he was saying was not about me, and that he was throwing it — me, actually — right in my face. It felt sort of brutal actually. That wasn't like him.

My Mr. Bigdick was understanding. My Mr. Bigdick was cumpassionate. My Mr. Bigdick was gentle. My Mr. Bigdick was kind. My Mr. Bigdick was tender. My Mr. Bigdick was sweet. My Mr. Bigdick helped me. My Mr. Bigdick understood. My Mr. Bigdick saw. My Mr. Bigdick felt. My Mr. Bigdick was anomalous. My Mr. Bigdick could see and feel things no one else can. He was like no one else. That's what made him so special.

And then I thought if he wasn't harassing me in a mean way, then what was he talking to me like that in that tone for? "Wrinkle the sheets together"? Did he really say that? I mean, like mean it? Is that how he really was? Is that what Mr. Bigdick thought was romantic? Not me. I didn't. And worst of all of, did he really think my calling him was only a ploy, I mean that I didn't really want to, you know, do him anyway? That would have been entirely false. I really wanted to. True: I had since France given, or begun, to give up hope. The airplanes riding into the WTC only built it up, or gave me the confidence to do what I had wanted. It wasn't a ploy in the sense that I didn't really care and was taking advantage of a tragedy to do something that I really wasn't interested in. I was interested. I was. I'm not like that. I don't do things I'm not really interested in. I'm sweet. I really am. I'm a good girl. I really am.

Then I thought after that: What if he meant exactly what he said, not sarcastically? What if he was just talking to me just the way it was. What if he was responding and agreeing with me, and just cutting through the bullshit, and really saying: If you're scared to be in New York, come on up to

my house and spend the weekend with me, Bettina? Yikes!
What if that was really it? What if he was inviting me up?
And what if I blew it then?

The more I thought about it, the more that that made
sense. He was using his humor to give me the knock-out
punch to cut out the funny business already. Like the crack
about him being a hundred thirty miles north. Why was I
calling, except that I was the one who was scared? Duh!
I get it now. The thing was, though, I never thought that
I'd go to his house. I mean, I am pretty sure he had a wife,
and how would that work? But, that's besides the point. I
was thinking, I think, that if something happened that he
would come down to New York and meet me, not that I'd
go upstate and meet him. It was too much like before when
he was my English teacher that way. At least to me it was.
I was scared; that part, that much, is true. And I wanted to
be with him. True, too. Only not there. Here. Here in New
York is where I wanted it to be. I wanted him to be in New
York and to do him here. That's what the problem was. Not
up there. I come from up there. It would be too much like
doing it at home. And like I said, that still feels kinda gross.
He was, after all, my English teacher. And that's the part I
sort of needed now to forget about. It's so cheesy like that:
Having sex with your old English teacher. It's not even original. If he came to New York with the billowing smoke, the
asbestos fumes, the twisted body parts' fuliginous scent in
the air, it would have been like the older protective man
hanging his cape over his young mistress' shoulders. That's
who I wanted to be: His special young mistress. That's who
I wanted. I couldn't be that up there. Up there I was just a
local girl who hadn't gotten over her crush on her English
teacher until he slept with her and probably they are found

out and it's in the papers and he ends up losing his job over it. I didn't want that for all sorts of reasons. I wanted it to be something special, not something so cheap and ordinary sounding. It is, but that's beside the point, too. I wanted it to be something I was going to remember forever my life by. Just doing it with your old English teacher is really kind of embarrassing. It's like so like *New York Post* and *Daily Mail* headlines. I wanted people to see us in New York City and be jealous and wonder and pass him a little handwritten note at a dinner table from across ours at a restaurant telling him what a lucky man he was to be with such a young girl. I wanted to be his princess. And when we went home to my apartment, I wanted him to cum and cum and cum inside me. And all the smoke in the world and all the dead people who died downtown would not have touched me then, nestled in the arms of my man, my mentor, and my literary master, Mr. Bigdick. And the truth is, I would have kept that note and written my own on the back of it telling Enright how I felt, about actually how lucky I felt I was actually to be with such a super-smart, super-sensitive, super-nice man myself like him. Because I was, or would have been. Because that was the truth about him. He was just great.

## 13

### *Thinking & memory; fiction & truth*

Thinking things over can be helpful. Thinking things over can be unhelpful. It just depends which way you look at it. Like everything. Everything is like something else. And that something else is like another thing. Eventually, everything comes back to itself. That's the way it is somehow. And somehow, everything always got back to me and Mr. Bigdick. It's just the way it was. Back in New York, after my junior year abroad and after the Eleventh of September, I was having sex with this little guy once; he was practically a dwarf, and I was reminded of Mr. Bigdick. Don't ask me how, but I was. There was like nothing in common with the two. The Dwarf, who was young and furry and very very built, even though he was very very tiny, too, had nothing in common you'd think with Mr. Bigdick. He was barely educated, he had a Southern accent, which I hate the most. People from the South sound like they grew up on plantations. They're all just as bad: Slaves and slaveholders. Nothing's really changed in the South as far as I can tell for hundreds of years. Whoops! There I go again, thinking like Mr. Bigdick. It seems that's all I do. His mind, his thinking, his way, his omnipresent aura is the path of gold, the exit on the highway, First Exit to Brooklyn, I always go to and get off on. He held views on things no sane, thinking person could believe anymore. I mean the Dwarf, not Mr. Bigdick. He didn't believe in black holes. He called all soda pop. He reckoned things and when he was about to cum, he was fixing to do it. It was all very comical of course. He didn't mean to be comical, and that's what made him so very funny to sleep with. He was a blast! Like a midget shot out of the barrel of a cannon, whew! His name was Egbert, and he did cum like a twenty-four pound cannonball. Shot after shot after shot. That's why I liked him. I did him more than once actually. I did him a bunch of times. But I broke it off. I have a thing about not being able to lock my fingers together with a man I'm fucking. It didn't bother me that he was not even five feet tall. Not at all. That was actually cool actually. Weird & Cool at the same time. Notice how unlikely pairs of things are often grouped, Mr. Bigdick said: Like Candy & Tobacco; sleeping yo-yos and coin-operated parking meters, both invented by a man named Duncan™. Whoops, there I go again! Thinking of him. Thinking like him, I should say. Weird & Cool. What bothered me was how small his fingers, how small his grip was. It made me feel like the man who was fucking me was a child by the size of his palms against my own, or, worse, pressed against my body. If you don't think it's creepy, try having sex with a guy whose hand is about the same size as a kid's whose colorful yellow, blue, and red smears of dried finger-painting should be praising his mom's Whirlpool® refrigerator instead of rubbing one of your A-cup size breasts. And for some reason, I don't know why, the Dwarf starting reminding me of Mr. Bigdick. He'd be doing me, making all sorts of dwarf noises, and I'd be cumming, and Mr. Bigdick would just come up in my mind. It wasn't even connected to anything really. He just came up there. I didn't like it. I didn't like it like that at all. So, even though the Dwarf really had a huge huge cock, which I did like, it was not just a cock, it was a monster, it was disproportionately large, I couldn't continue seeing him. I had to break it off. The hands part, even though it felt creepy and gross to me, like I was like Florence Nightingale sleeping with a pre-schooler, it was like that, I could put up with it. But thinking about Mr. Bigdick while the Dwarf's enormously huge cock was in me going up and down, no way! I couldn't put up with that part after a coupla weeks when it started happening. I tried to make it go away. But it didn't. It only grew worse. I tried not to hurt his feelings, but he seemed really really happy. Who wouldn't be, getting to fuck me? And what were his chances he was going to have anyone even close to like me again? Pretty nil. Or, maybe I was wrong. I shouldn't think so much of myself. He definitely knew how to handle a lady. Which tells me he was a lot more experienced than I'm giving him credit for. Some people are just thankful in life. Egbert, I tell you, he was one of them. There was a gentle heart in that one. But I couldn't in good conscience keep fucking him night after night after night and cumming and cumming and cumming and be thinking, with my eyes shutting, of Mr. Bigdick. It's not right. It's just not right. So, I broke it off without really telling him the real reason why. That's standard practice in most relationships. If you tell people the real reasons why, they leave sort of hurt and stunted. Why not just leave things on the sunnier side and say you need to move on and blame it on yourself? Everyone knows it's a lie, but, sort of like calling another Senator whose views you know are totally fucked up and fascist *my esteemed colleague*, it gets the job done without it getting overtly personal which isn't really necessary and hardly worth the extra energy involved going about it that way. The Dwarf was really decent about it. He even sent me a dozen roses the next day and said he would remember me the rest of his life. That was sweet. I like that. Sweetness is always a plus, a bonus, in my book.

That's what I get for thinking things over. Memories. I've thought things over before and gotten nowhere. And I've thought things over and figured things out. Mr. Bigdick was an enigma to me. Part of me wanted to figure him out. Part of me just wanted to forget him. A lot of me just wanted to do him, I think, because he seemed so unique. Memories. What are they? Who are they? And where do they come from? It seems like some of them are so real; it feels like what you're dreaming about is happening. Take *Bettina's World*. It's just make-up of course, but I feel it in my bones, I feel in my heart, I feel it in my cunt. It's strange: I don't see it with my eyes the way I see seeing things with my eyes, but inside them. Like it's inside my head, but a part of it that isn't about thinking or understanding or making sense of anything at all. Like the way when you see a terrible traffic accident, you see the horror of it inside you. My feelings about Mr. Bigdick went the other way around than seeing seeing. They were inside feelings. That's the way I saw him. When I saw the farmhouses, I could feel me and him inside the barn even though you couldn't see us. That's the way a memory is. You feel it in the inside. Even though I couldn't point a finger anywhere really, and my head seems the least likely spot actually, a memory feels like a total physical reality inside you. My brain may be the thing used for holding the memory or taking it to begin with. But it works like a camera. It takes the moment, but it doesn't go through the feeling of it. Cameras don't feel; they take. The looker feels it. In a memory, the person is both the taker and the looker. And in my picture of me and Mr. Bigdick, I felt like both. That's what's interesting. In my idea of *Bettina's World*, it's a fantasy. But it feels no different to me than something that actually happened. If it's inside me, it's inside me; if it's outside me, it's outside. Mr. Bigdick, gosh, he felt so real, I was afraid I could never get him out. Memories. I've got some pretty amazing ones. One of the ones I like best, you guessed it, no surprise, is with me and Mr. Bigdick.

One day, during school, this was 7th period of course before he kicked me out of it, Mr. Bigdick was thrashing around in his closet, the one with the *Christina's World* poster on it. He was doing this before I came in evidently, and I just gave him the usual, "Hi, Mr. Bigdick. How are you this fine, fine afternoon?" *So much crap, so much crap in here*, he said. *In where?* I said. I can be like that. I'm not really spacey or a flake at all really. I just liked to hear him talk, that's all. This CLOSET is filled with stuff, stuff from YEARS ago. I can't believe how much STUFF I've got in here. He kept emphasizing his words like they were capital letters like that. It was a parody of the way people are of course. He did that kind of stuff all the time. Which made him cool. You just had to know him though. If you knew him, you'd understand. *Your stuff?* I asked him. *No*, he said, *the Blue Meanies. I see*, I said. He just wanted to talk himself, not that he really minded all the things he was pulling out of his closet and dumping on the floor. There was a Pictionary® game, lots of half-used up stacks of paper plates, Styrofoam® plates and cups, a radio or tape player or something like that, and the remains of all kinds of leftover projects from students like decks of handmade cards, and sugar cube dice, and key rings with big fake cardboard keys hanging from them. All kinds of things. And then he pulled out Scrabble®. Scrabble®! I love Scrabble®. *You want?* he said. *To play?* I replied. And the next thing I knew we were playing it. In school. It's so amazing! Can you believe it, my favorite game? With Mr. Bigdick, my favorite teacher!

It was the game of my life. I'll never forget it. It sounds like a dream. He went first. And I swear to God, this is what happened. He got a seven-letter word right off. That's a fifty point bonus on top of the fact that it's a double word score to begin with. He spelled it out V-A-G-I-N-A-S laying each squarish wooden tile down with a snapping sound against the board. The S was a blank. I had the S and so when it was my turn, I just went vertically P-E-N-I-S. I know I could have used the blank S off the end of *vaginas*, and it was a waste of an S, but it made the board look like a giant hard cock sticking out to the left from the start. *If I had had your "P,"* he said, having loaded up a fresh rack of tiles after his turn and mine, *I could have done "pervert."* Oh, well, I said, *I guess you'll just have to wait for one.* He did *peeved*, going down, instead. It was incredible. The whole game went on like this. I once asked him, because I wasn't sure, *Is "cum" a word? It's a total waste of a U unless it's the end of the game and you need to dump it or get stuck with it.* "Dump," "stuck," get it? That's how he was! When you knew Mr. Bigdick the way I knew Mr. Bigdick, you knew it was always about playing games. He was always playing them! Games inside games inside games. I mean how many people do you know who when they're playing Scrabble® are also spelling out in their minds what they're saying in their heads as a kind of double answer to a single idea about using a "u" in a word? Mr. Bigdick could. Mr. Bigdick did. He was about something else that most people would never guess the meaning of if they were shown it right in front of themselves ten times or ten million. He just had a sense of humor. That's all. Most people, you'll have to agree, really don't have one. They really don't.

Then, let's see, the next thing that happened, he pounced on me. Yup. Right then and there. And I'm like, whoah tiger! Hold on, big boy! Yup. Knock them tiles over. What happened is more like this: I'd just put down the word *dong*, snapping the mahogany tiles against the board, and he literally reaches across the board and dumps my rack. His fingers skimmed mine because I had a couple of letters in my hands where I was taking them from the boxtop overturned next to us face-down for replenishing our depleted rows of seven. *Go again, Bettina, go again*, he says. I tell him I can't, that I just went. And he says again, *Go again, Bettina, go again*. Of course I'm thinking that I can't go ahead again because it's his turn, that it'd be breaking the rules. And I think then next: That's exactly what he wants: Me to break the rules. Picture me sitting Indian style on the floor, we both are. I feel the little closed flaps in the front of my cunt a little bit moist, just a wee bit, and I adjust my cross-legged position to feel them separate more a little bit. I assure it that that's what it is. It feels good, and re-adjust my knees still more just a little bit more to open it up, the V. Maybe a vagina's called a vagina because it opens up with its shape, who knows? And without a V it's like angina, a little heart attack. I don't know, but that's how I felt. A little horny heart attack. I'm a little bit afraid, I'm a lot afraid actually. The bell's going to ring in like five minutes and, I've got Studio Art next, even though we're not doing anything there except drawing hands. We'd been drawing and drawing those Escher hands drawing themselves out the wazzoo for like two solid weeks.

The left hand drawing the left hand drawing the left hand. It gets boring after a while. We're both lefties, Mr. Bigdick and me. It was good, Studio Art, but it was boring. *I've got Studio Art* next, I tell him. *Sixty hands will be pounding at the door in five minutes, Bettina*, he replied. It's hard to know sometimes what's a game and what's not. Then he picks up the board by one corner and all the words *vagina, cunt, pussy, orgasm, cum, peeved, dick, rape, boner, fur, lemon, slot, yoni, gash, slice, mule, toothpick, whip, grip, omo, bedhop* — they all come tumbling down the northwest corner to the floor. I can see, even though he's sitting like Chief Sitting Bull or Custer Peace Pipe that he's as big as Gibraltar now. I catch a glimpse of the door before it happens and see the square glass window to his classroom door is covered with paper taped to it. Very strange. It never is. I do a Seven-Eleven. It's named after a Big Gulp. Which is a blow job. It's a giant soda, in case you're from the South, and don't know it. In case you're Egbert and you get your dwarfish little hands on this someday in your travels and travails, you'll understand. He busts up the railroad, which is another way of putting: Mr. Bigdick undoes his zipper, because it's like separating the ties on a train track, and pulls out his big white dick. He doesn't really have a big dick. A man named that can't really have a big one. I'm just kidding there! Of course he does! It's not just a cock. It's a monster! Did I say that already? C'mon, cowboy, and lasso me with that barnthang of yours. I'm just kidding again. No, he really does. And grabs the back of my head, me and him still sitting like two Indians, and puts my head in his lap over it. Our knees are almost touching and it's a bit uncumfortable, bending at the base of the spine like that, even though I am quite flexible. In addition to playing flute, school newspaper editor, and running track, I did dance for eleven years. En pointe! En pointe! En pointe! The cursed sounds of a Balanchine despot, a big-balled, big-thighed homo who spent most of his time looking at his own marvelously sculpted body in gray tights instead of ours. That's just criminal! Any one of us would have sucked him off, I'm sure of it. But homos like him, they're not interested. They want another homo like themselves to do it. That's why they call it *queer*. Because it's queer to want that. To want someone for cumpany to do it who's really just yourself instead of someone who's different to do it for a change. Who'd want to suck off himself more instead of having a little fourteen year old do it like me? Isn't that a lot more exciting? So I go down on him. That was my first blow-job. I loved it! It was like having the exhaust of a vacuum cleaner blown up your ass except in reverse. Instead of gas, it was liquid. Instead of anal, it was oral. I could see then, looking over it from the past into the future, where my original predilection, my disposition toward anal came from. From Mr. Bigdick. Everything came from him. My mouth, my lips, my chin is overflowing with his cum, Mr. Bigdick's. I can't believe it! I can't honestly to God actually believe it! I've got Mr. Bigdick's cum flowing from my mouth. Hallelujah! You can go over Niagara Falls in a barrel. You can land a man on the moon. You can put the apex on the Great Pyramid's top. But who's the one who sucked off Mr. Bigdick in AP? Me. Me did. Me, Bettina. You, Jane. Oh, whatever. I was so happy. I was so excited. I was so full of glee. He reached from inside his baggy sweater and pulled out, neatly folded, a stack of brown paper towels. *They're coarse, but effective*, he said, handing me one. And my mind clicked like time's own camera and I saw it all. From way before when I had said *fine, fine afternoon,*

*Mr. Bigdick* that afternoon he had been planning, plotting, arranging it all. His desultory rummaging about through his coat closet — all a set-up, a charade, a farce, a front, a ruse. Oh, he was so brilliant. To make the occasion of love look like happenstance. To make my first real live blow-job look like serendipity. The games, cups, plates, junk on the floor. The paper on the window. The game of Scrabble® suggested like an afterthought. It was all so brilliant and musical, like jazz. For me. That's what I liked best about it. He did it all for me. There was no limit to the games his impromptu mind would make up and play. We were all tiles to Mr. Bigdick. He was the Scrabblemaster. And I was the blank, his clean slate, his *tabula rasa*, his open field, his little fresh cunt he could write any letter on. B. C. V. It didn't matter. I would be any letter in the box he chose. So long as he chose me, that's all that counted.

Fiction, truth. Non-fiction, whatever. Whatever people call it, what does it matter? So long as the feelings are real and it gets me off, doesn't that count, too? It does. Listen, there are all sorts of memories. So many of them belong in the dump. So take them there. Let the Dead bury the Dead. Do you want the Dead living in your house? I don't want them in mine. I only want the Living living in my cunt. I only want the Living pumping me there. And Mr. Bigdick, even if he never touched me, OK, so I got carried away with the whole Scrabble® thing, OK, so I'm the Scrabblemaster here, OK so I'm the mistress, OK, so it got me off now just imagining it, OK, so let's just say for argument's sake that his thorny talons grazed my fingers once, I could still tell that Mr. Bigdick was a real live pumper. You just could tell. If you had a sense for it. People who take pictures with cameras, they have no imagination. They take a picture and their memories are done. They fill up album after album after album and name each one on the binder back a year 1956, 1957, 1958, etcetera. It's a march toward death if you ask me. It's not creative. It doesn't make anything. It doesn't make anybody think. And people with photo albums, who throws them away? Nobody. Nobody does. They don't have any memories at all actually because they've taken so many pictures.

My pictures of me and Mr. Bigdick are infinite. I can arrange and re-arrange them. Like tiles. Depending on my mood. Depending on the day. Depending on who I'm fucking. Or not. I'm the photographer. Not the camera. That's where so many people go wrong. Like a pen in the old-fashioned world running out of ink. Does that really stop the story-telling? Only if you do. In fact, everybody knows how much people don't know because of writing anyway. Before, they used to memorize the *Odyssey*. Fourteen thousand men watched a Greek play like *Oedipus Rex* together and all of them knew Homer by heart. They didn't know much else, but so what. They knew a lot. They knew what would amount to in this day and age the breadth of a PhD scholar. Or more today, take cumputer chips. People think about how much memory their cumputers have, but that's only because we don't have them anymore. We think of memories like something fixed and permanent. That's just an iceberg. And the truth is, even icebergs do move. Take Beethoven or Mozart, when these guys played, these guys played. And people came not to hear how exactly exact one of them could rip through the *Moonlight,* but what it would sound like that night. Music was a skeleton written down to be played off of. When it was written down, it was just a version. Nothing more than that. Making it the same all the time kills all the life in it. What makes live music sound so good? That it sounds like it's just being made up, that it's fresh, that it's new. Not that it's exactly the same as it always was. It's just about a sad lack of our having real memories today. Like me. I was totally freaked out because I lost more than twenty pages of this, right here! That's right! Right here! And I went through my cumputer files for three days pulling out all the broken pieces. I wanted to put together my Mr. Bigdick story just the way it was. I believed it was gone, my story about Mr. Bigdick. I believed in my cumputer, that it was my memory. It's like believing my cumputer is making my story. And if I can't get it back, it's my failure. That's just plain stupid. I remember how one 7th period conversation me and Mr. Bigdick, I like to say it that way, it doesn't sound so poetic, were talking about the life of a writer. We talked about things like this all the time. And he told me about D. H. Lawrence, how D. H. Lawrence would sit by the riverbank and sometimes a wind would come and blow all his work away. He'd just start up again writing where he was, he said. Now that's about memory. Memory is creative. Memory makes. I tried for those three or four days to put the pieces of my lost twenty pages back together again. That's like putting together bits of dinosaur bones and believing, once you've added the plaster and plastic and paint, that when you've got the whole extinct monster framed out it'll roar in your living room. It just won't happen. It never will. D. H. Lawrence wrote 3,000 words a day; he was always creating. That's what it's about. If the wind, if some electro-magnetic storm comes and blows your work away, just begin again. Just begin where you left off. That's all you can do. Or not. You can choose to reconstruct what you've lost; you can choose to rebuild it. But that's not art, that's not writing;

that's archaeology. That's moving backwards instead of forwards. That's like believing you can't know yourself unless
you fully understand your origins. Well, that's just wrong.
Just accept where you are and go. If you've got one leg and
you find yourself in the middle of a speeding four-lane highway, it is no time to reflect how or why you lost that limb.
It's time to move across the highway. And, basically, we are
all all of us one-leggers in the middle of a four-lane highway.
Either get hit by the oncumming traffic or move on. That's
why it makes sense Jewish people get buried no later than a
day after they die. You keep picking and picking and picking
at the brains of JFK for a week and it doesn't change the fact
that he's dead. Let's move on LBJ! And that's what I did. But,
I've got to confess, with knowing Mr. Bigdick, it was very
very hard. He was such a big big influence. He made me see
so much of the world through his intellectual binoculars; I
didn't know how to forget him. I've had such a hard time
throwing out memories of him. Taking him to the dump has
been next to impossible. It's so hard. He was so big. Gosh!
It's one thing to be the pharmacist, but it's another to fill the
teaspoon full of your own over-the-counter medicine and
drink it. Yuck! But, boy, do I really like the taste of cum
though!

For like four years since Mr. Bigdick's class I did a lot of
fucking, thinking it would be like getting rid of my memories of him, or forgetting him. But it's always turned out
to be the opposite. For some reason I just can't get his fla-
vor out of my mouth. He's like a cough syrup, the one with
dextromethorphan in it, that's a narcotic practically; and I
find myself, now that I'm over eighteen and, so long as I
have my I.D. with me proving that I'm that, going back and
back for it at the drugstore and buying it. I ought to come

out with my own brand of it: Mr. Bigdick's Cough Remedy. You hooked me, Mr. Bigdick. Big time. In class, when I was your student, you hooked me. Big. I'm a Mr. Bigdick junkie. And basically, in addition to my studies, that's all I've done: Looked for men with big dicks for four years. But none is bigger than his, none is better than his; none is sweeter, none is finer.

# 14

## *Sexual history*

Gosh! When you have a memory like mine, the world is a very busy place. I was hanging out on the Palisades Parkway one day with this guy I was doing; he was counting hawks, and I thought maybe I should look old Mr. Bigdick up again. It was around October, November and there were what this guy was calling kettles in the sky. They were filled with thousands and thousands of hawks gathering together for the big migration south. They do that, hawks. I didn't know, but this guy I was with would go up there off the vista by the hot dog restaurant and keep a tally. He only brought one stool to sit on, which I thought pretty inconsiderate. But, like I've said, young guys know zilch or next to zilch about courtesy. This was like a month, maybe two after the Arabs crashed their planes into the WTC; maybe it was the year after that, I can't be sure. Honestly, I don't even know for sure what this guy's name was. Although I do remember what his little pecker was like. It was pretty little. The skinniest little thing I'd ever let pick its way inside me. C'mon you little pecker! C'mon in! There's room for anybody. And maybe I was just feeling nostalgic heading north on the Palisades there when I all of a sudden I told this guy Jay or something that I had to get back, I mean to Harrisford. We were just outside the city we'd just come from, and Harris-ford's not that far from there, and it was his car, and he was of course driving. I don't know why I was with him. Some guys are filler. I call them packing peanuts. They keep little old delicate me packed safe and cumfortable and make a terrible mess when they spill out of their box and they're so hard to get rid of anyway once they're in your life. He was like that. Like packing peanuts. I probably have a thing for anything made of Styrofoam®, and told this Jay or whatever guy who was keeping these tallies of species he was, that it was time to go. We stayed for another half hour because he had the keys and then he did what I told him to. That's the way it most always works. Once a guy's in your pants, they'll drive to the moon for you. And all you have to do is offer to pay the tip every once and while and they're happy as house dogs. They're pretty simple, most guys. We got to the mid-point, where the toll is, and I changed my mind. *Jay or whatever, let's go back*, I said. And he did. I wasn't with him that much longer. He never said no to anything. Do you want corned beef? Do you want decaf? Do you want marzi-pan? Do you want mahi mahi? Do you want McDonald's? Jay or whatever never said no to anything. So there wasn't even a conversation. And plus he had one of those needle in the haystack type of dicks that wasn't worth the search. It was just filler. I don't know why I was with him anyway.

Having established that ornithology isn't my strong suit, I started doing the cumplete opposite. No, that does not mean I started fucking a chicken farmer. I have my limits. I don't think I'd ever let a guy's cock into me whose job it was to pull out chicken feathers all day. That's just really gross. Where do all the feathers go? Pillows? I just don't want to think about it. And I don't want some chicken dick guy sliding in and out of me meanwhile while I'm thinking about what he does with pulled out chicken feathers. That's the gross part. The job part, I can handle. It's when you start thinking about what else they do while they're doing you that you start thinking about why you're doing what you are. I want my memory working on things I like, if I can help it. Let's say a guy's doing me and he's this great, famous novelist, like the dwarf I was doing Egbert Starr was. That's an easy one. I think of him sitting all morning with his beautiful foreign born wife asleep in silky sheets behind him and he's been up since before the first whisper of dawn spoke writing about how much he loves her. I could do him in half a heartbeat. That's the kind of man I was destined to remember. That's the kind of man I was born to imagine. What I meant by the opposite of Jay or something was the guy after him kept track literally of nothing. You could say he was lavish, but I say he just didn't care. Like he'd go somewhere with me and pay like he hadn't thought of it. He was older of course, too, so that might have had something to do with it. I guess what I mean was nothing seemed to have any value to him. It was weird because you could also say he was generous. It was right around Valentine's Day actually that he was doing me. And he gave me a gold necklace, eighteen karat, with a fire opal the size of a thumbnail hanging from it. That's just overkill unless he really meant it. But we were not in love. Clearly. That's something you give someone when you're in love. Not when a box of chocolates, or a dozen roses, or a dinner at an upscale Tibetan restaurant would do perfectly well. It was a dead giveaway that he didn't really care. When I gave it back to him, he wrote me a check for it. That was really weird. How do you interpret that? Thank you? Now his name I remember, but I'm not going to even bother. And

what I did with the check, because check's you've got to realize are not cash, they create a decision the recipient must
then make, because no one just tears up seven Ben Franklins
and one U. S. Grant, I'm going to keep that part between
me and myself. Let's just say it was soon after that I was
sporting a pair of nice Joan & David ankle boots. But I'm
not saying what I did with this guy's paper check. God! I say
*God*, he was a paper dick. He really turned me off.

Somewhere on my wheel of fortune, I did a high schooler
just like I was once. He was just the puppy dog of gratitude.
He came from Bensonhurst, had an accent like you wouldn't
believe, Brooklyn to the core, but good. He hadn't even had
a cup of coffee when I met him. He didn't drink even Coke®.
He was pure, like he was devout if he had had one of those
broad-brimmed Amish hats. You see those pale-skinned
lads standing in LaGuardia with their bearded fathers and
just want to take those suspenders off their shoulders. Boy!
They're really something, the simple, creaking horse-and-
buggy folk. But this kid, Liebowitz, he took to caffeine like
fish to the ocean. He couldn't get enough of it. Starbucks™,
Dean & Deluca™, Zabar's™, Cooper's™, Xando™, New
World Coffee™, Timothy's World Coffee™ any streetcorner
with a java joint on it, he wanted to go into. He was so
sweet. I liked drinking mochas on Third with him more than
being done by him, quite honestly. At that age, when you're
sixteen and the woman's like twenty-one, twenty-two, it's
just so Flaubert, it's a whole *Sentimental Education* kind of
thing. To be a mentor, now that was really something special. And I felt, instead of taking and taking all the time, I
was giving. Truthfully, he barely got into me before he came.
Actually, three out of four times he came before he popped
his dick even in. I just patted him on the back every time it

happened and we'd go out for a latté. Teenagers. One thing I learned from him is not to take the things they do personally. He started fading, got wrapped up with college applications, the school play. When he started wondering about sexual identity, I saw the velvet curtain about to fall. He had to find some things out for himself. Alone. That meant drugs. Experimentation. He was done with me. I didn't mind. It wasn't like being used. It was like helping someone find out about themselves. Being a stepstool. I was just there when he needed to grow. I gave him a sack of Our Planet™ organic coffee beans, a French glass coffee press, and a box of one dozen lubricated lambskin condoms coated with spermicide the last time we met. *Good luck, Franklin,* I said. *I'll never forget you, Bettina,* he said with steadfast earnestness to me. *Shhh!* I said. *You have a sweet life. Now go!* And he did. I watched him walk away with the canvas I ♥ COFFEE bag and gifts I gave him inside it to the end of the block where there was another Starbucks kitty-korner to another one on the southeast side and go into it solo this time. The whole experience took my breath away. I, too, felt like I was growing up a bit. Even if that bit was only a small bit, or a bit of a bit.

Another guy was a total Polaroid® freak. He was totally fucked up. He wore one turquoise contact lens and one blue one. He took Polaroids of everything, wherever it was. He'd sit in Father Demo Square and take a Polaroid® of just a plain guy eating a bagel. No big deal. But then he'd take a Polaroid® of a someone being written a parking ticket for an expired parking meter. The real problem I had is he thought his pictures were interesting. He took me up to his rooftop with his Polaroid® camera and took a picture of the skyline. *See all the water towers across the skyline of the city?* he

said. And then the Polaroid® camera would go: Chhkgrrr.
And out it'd come, a picture of basically nothing. That was
the problem. We'd be fucking and I'd say: *Take a picture
of me, take a picture of me cumming!* And he'd slip out his
dick, whether it'd be from my ass or my cunt, and go get his
camera. This little fuck-head would come back like ten minutes later with all sorts of pictures, three or four of them not
fully vivid. A Polaroid® of Crest® toothpaste. A Polaroid®
of clothes in a hamper. A Polaroid® of a box of Kleenex®.
I noticed that a lot of the things he took happened to be
name brand things, things like with registered trademarks.
Marko, I told him, if I had an ® on my cunt, would you take
a picture of your cum creeping out of me? He didn't get it.
The guy really was sort of a creep. I think he probably was
Asperger's. I mean he had like almost no emotional tone in
his responses, like everything was the same fact as another
thing. At first it sounded very intelligent, very detached, very
observer *I Am A Camera* sort of Andy Warhol's-In-Your-
Living-Room/Andy Warhol's-Not-In-Your-Living-Room
sort of way where the *he is* part and the *he is not* part aren't
really that important. But then, when I realized when Marko
was fucking me in my pussy he wasn't any more interested
in fucking me in my pussy than when he was fucking me in
my asshole, I realized it didn't make a bit of difference to
me if I was even fucking Marko. *Fuck, Marko, am I getting
autistic like you? No*, he said. Just like another fact. That's
fucked. A good cock, he had. Held onto his cum long, and it
was juicy. But fucking Marko was like being tapped all day
by a water-clock or something. I should have figured it out
sooner, right away. But I didn't. He'd put Ravel on, fourteen
and-a-half minutes of *Bolero* monotony and cum every time
at the crescendo like twelve minutes into it. When I caught

him taking a Polaroid® at the R-rating sign up close on a movie poster once, I thought I'd had it. For me, in retrospect, it was a turning point. The poster itself was great. Some Amazon type woman very décolleté with a big green anaconda type snake wrapped around her waist and boobs. He didn't even notice or pay attention to that part. He was just sort of kneeling up close to the poster with the up-close latch on the Polaroid® camera slid over to the left, taking a close-up picture of the R-rating R in the rating box at the bottom of the poster. The only other music he liked was Philip Glass. I like him too in a way, in the background, but not forever. Not the same track played on repeat a whole weekend. The different colored contact lens bit I never got. It didn't fit in with the rest of his character. But I didn't ask. I just didn't ask. It would have ended up being one of those *yes* or *no* type answers that it didn't make a difference if he answered *yes* or *no* to or not.

I did this homeless guy once. A bum. Just once. I was drunk. I didn't even realize who he was, that he was homeless until the morning the next day. If it means doing somebody twice if you have sex two times, then I guess it means I did him twice actually. Because he did me in the morning also. If it means being in the same bed with somebody once, then just one time. I didn't even remember the night. I only knew he'd done me because there was a skin on the floor. That's my own term I sometimes use for condoms. They're gross but *condoms* doesn't sound gross. So, let's call them something gross like the way they are. And I came up with skins. That's perfect, I thought. So, I do. Now look at it like this: A homeless guy goes back with a drunk college girl and he fucks her with a skin. What's the likelihood of that? Less than zero, I'd say. But there it was: A skin on the floor full of cum. And when he was on top of me again in the morning, after I'd gotten up to pee and stepped next to the skin from the night before, he had already peeled open another foil and rolled it over his erect penis. He did it like he was making a fresh cup of tea, peeling the corner of the square package open by the dotted line with an aloof look of habit. It was indeed for him I could see a matter of course. What made his station in life obvious was the huge sack of soda and beer cans in the corner of my room. When it was over and he had done me a second time, and I gave the verbal cues that it was time for him to depart, he gave me a sorry look. It was like when you do make a cup of tea for someone for the first time and you don't know exactly how they take it sort of look. Sort of a sorry look if it's not quite the way to please you look. If he had ever mentioned me his name, I don't recall it. I thought: Maybe he's so diligent about skins because he believes he's protecting himself from me, rather than his being decent by protecting me from himself. After all, homeless people you'd think are promiscuous. Yes, I looked myself in the mirror on that. He came. He rolled the skin almost immediately off his penis, tied the end of it in a knot to prevent any leakage, and lay it beside the other one on the floor. *Good-bye*, he said. *Thank you*, I said. His cans rattled as he left, and I was glad it was over.

And what else? I did do a few schoolteachers. I have a nose for them. One in particular. Lewis. We'd met at the bar on Third Street off Bleeker, or maybe it was the Nightbird on Amsterdam uptown between 114th and 115th. I don't really remember that part. It was during a time me and a friend were into partying and a lot of ass-fucking both of us. It was like a fad practically between the two of us. And I met this Social Studies teacher. He was totally into Apple cumputers. I've got a Dell. Oh, well! But give me a break! Lewis was fucking me hard and still talking, I mean literally actually talking, about Apple cumputers. He'd be talking about this peripheral and that peripheral and I'd be like in my head: I'm gonna cum in a sec, Lewis, and I don't want your Apple cumputer overlay in my brain while I'm cumming, thank you! And he was paranoid. He thought just because he used Macs, that the administration was out to get him. Really. He had this whole conspiracy theory going on about viruses and worms and espionage and Mary Magdalene and the Catholic Church. He somehow connected Bill Gates with some global organization he called the Illuminati who were waiting until the year 2023 to take over the whole world and render us all robotic automatons. Steve Jobbs was like the archangel of individual freedom to him. And Steve Jobbs and Macs were the only way we were going to be set free from what Lewis called the Draconian rule of the Illuminati. It was all too much sometimes. Interesting, but sometimes too much for me to believe. Or want to. Anyway, Lewis came like a horse. How he'd ever gotten to be a schoolteacher and not fired was beyond me. I was honest with him and we talked about it. *Macs*, he said. *If you own a Mac, they can't catch you. Have you ever heard of anyone ever getting a virus who owns a Mac?* Wow, I've picked up some strange ones in my life, and I'm putting him on my short list! Lewis, well, besides Macs and conspiracy theory, he knew how I liked my ass worked. And I preferred him there quite honestly than the front. But all the chatter about Macs going on in my ear, constantly, all the time, whispered right behind me in my ear, I tried to remember what was useful of course, but I didn't even have the money to buy a quarter of the stuff he mentioned anyway. It was on, shall I say, my periphery? And just mention of that word to Lewis, and off he was muttering about the latest Mac-Gadget. Even when Lewis himself was cumming, he'd being going on about Macs. I couldn't even imagine him teaching at a school. I really couldn't. He was a madman. Nice. But a total Apple-bonkers madman.

One of the most ridiculous fucks I ever had in my life was with Nihil Liebermann, President of Laurent Sternes College, which I'd thought was like a Swiss finishing school for boys in Manhattan. Oh, my God, what a freak! I met him outside Lincoln Center one Friday night. He was coming out of something I didn't even go to. And there's a limousine waiting. I was probably half-drunk so I ask this man in a bow tie and top hat for a light. I don't even smoke. I don't even have a cigarette. And he starts this totally off-beat but friendly banter, and I'm thinking: Is he hitting on me? We get to talking about where he's from, where I'm from, and we grew up in the same exact town! Just about down the road from each other. Now we both live in New York! How about it? That cements it. The limo driver opens the door for me and him, and the next thing I know I'm dining with him at A la Fourchette, an incredible French restaurant, at a private table. He's very debonair, very smart. He's not really that smart; he's full of lots of affectation actually, one of those Old World Jews who thinks he's a New World Teddy Roosevelt. But I liked, because I do, his attention. Almost nothing turns me on more than the attention of an older man. It's almost one-way, his way. Simone de Beauvoir, Jean-Paul Sartre. How the mentor/mentee relationship involving romance and books is dead today. Very interesting. Very interesting. And Hannah Arendt. And Else

Lasker-Schüler. He was very very impressive in his pompous way. Nihil, I finally said, do you want to sleep with me? And that guy had a hunk of meat, let me tell you. I hunk of limp, dead meat. It was like a limp dead smelly vulture hung on a meat hook. It was about that time that I began formulating my theory about Jews and their cocks. He had this pied à terre, whatever that meant, on West End Avenue that was just perfect for me. It was basically only a few blocks from classes. So it was very convenient to sleep there. Nihil'd call things normally what other people wouldn't: The *latch*, the *porter, la pièce de résistance*. He was very impressed that I spoke French. He told me a very sad tale about his mother I won't even mention, an unnecessary ploy to evoke sympathy to bed me the first night we did it. I didn't need that. It was sort of a turn off actually. I was hungry for his coat-tails. I was hungry to please myself. I was hungry to get in. I was hungry, very hungry for attention. I always am, I seem. He was ridiculous, though. He'd be trying to stuff his giant baggy cock into my wet pussy, a total no-go, with both his hands and telling me, *au même temps*, at the same time, that is, how he believed the American public high school was a mote on the eye of the Republic. That's the way he talked, or referred to things. The *Union* rather than the country. *Antebellum*, instead of before the Civil War. Or *Weltanshauung* instead of just saying what his outlook on life was. It got to be annoying, nauseating, actually. Not just the stuffing with the hands bit that never worked out by the way, but the whole language thing he had going. And his accent. Oh, God. Like Burgess Meredith in *Batman* as the Penguin. Yyyyesss! Yyyyesss! Gimme a break! That's not that how Jews talk! That's not a Jew! He couldn't even fuck me good.

What am I talking about? He couldn't even fuck me period.
I won't take that from anybody. Old baldy with the Fireside
Chat voice, he was the living picture of one Dutch citizen in
Boer-ruled South Africa going yaw yaw yaw in a pith helmet to another one under a tarp going yaw yaw yaw to him
about the injustice of colonial rule in South Africa, while
being poured ice water from a glass pitcher by a local black
guy. It was just totally disgusting. Total bullshit. By the end
of it, I really couldn't stomach that man's yaw-yawing about
Anna Akhmatova or whoever it was was the greatest poet
in the world while he was trying to stuff me with his giant
baggy cock. It never got in. Even with both hands working
it. It was big. I have to admit that part. But flabby. Yuck. So,
I dumped him. Intellectuals in bow ties, I'll never let one of
their baggy cocks touch me again, so long as I live.

All these guys got me thinking. What was so special about
Mr. Bigdick? Well, he had a big dick. OK. What else? Well,
it smelled big. OK. What else? I can be very self-reflective at
times. But I have to push myself there. But once I'm there:
Wham! I'm like a gigantic tsunami that runs past you and
then sweeps back over itself like a fine-toothed comb. And I
asked myself: Bettina, what did all these guys I fucked have
that Mr. Bigdick did not? Little dicks. Thin dicks. Dicks
that didn't get up. And dicks that never went down. Dicks
that blew it in a coupla quick, short breaths. And dicks that
huffed and puffed on forever. Some were like feathers; some
like tanks. Some smooth; some scraped. Some sweet. Some
salty. Some sour. Some were narrow; some fat. Yellow, white,
brown, and black. Dicks. That's what it's all about. It's all
about dicks I realized. And Mr. Bigdick's, it was a classic. An
American classic. It was a root. It was strong, ample, fair. It
was enduring, capable, rich. It was mine. I had to have it.

It was an American original. And there ain't much of that left here 'round these parts anymore, pardner! Nope. Not much of that 'round here at all anymore, I'm afraid. Whew! I wanted him.

## 15

### *Busted*

When I got the news about Mr. Bigdick, I was right in the middle of fucking these three Asian guys. Not literally in the middle of it, but when I heard about him that's who I was fucking those days. Even though they weren't really, I called them the three brothers Ng. They didn't even look the same. McCurdy. Park. Fitzgerald. Surnames. Last names of the three of them. Didn't even know one another. Hairless but sinewy. A Korean. A Mick. An American. Can you guess which one? One of them was pure. Two mutts. Can you guess which one? One liked poetry. Two liked math. Can you guess which one? All three: Meat-eaters. All three: College-educated. Between 19 and 32. If Park is the youngest, and McCurdy is not the oldest, what is Fitzgerarld's age? Can you guess which one? Abacus abacus on the wall, who's the sexiset Asian guy of them all? And then out of the blue I heard from Xsu-Xsu, of all people; we hadn't talked since practically the summer after high school, who told me that Mr. Bigdick had been busted. That was a shock, a real shock. I've got all this Asian dick in me, and she calls me up out of the blue and tells me Mr. Bigdick himself got busted at the high school. It was like total SWAT. See, they've got cumputers, and it was after there was this cumplaint by some student teacher, by this chick from Austria. I practically puked when I heard from where she was from: Europe. Apparently, she was Viennese. Apparently, her visiting visa was about to be burned out. Apparently, she was trying to buy more time in the U.S. Apparently, she signed up for some teacher education program at some cummunity college. Apparantly, she got a placement at Harrisford High School. Apparently, she thought it would save her skin. Apparently, she wanted to marry an American. Apparently, Mr. Bigdick had the hots for her. Apparently, he bought her some German candy. Apparently, she took it. Apparently, he asked her out for coffee. Apparently, she went. Apparently, he sent emails. Apparently, she got them. Apparently, she had given him her address. Apparently, he asked her out for dinner. Apparently, they went. Apparently, he liked her. Apparently, she liked him. Apparently, apparently. Yeah! Way to go, Mr. Bigdick! Way to go! Hitting on the local Eurotrash. Apparently, a cumplaint was filed. Apparently, they pounced on his cumputer. Apparently, a charge was filed. Apparently, he was arrested. Apparently, I know what the problem was. Apparently, Mr. Bigdick was just a nice guy. Apparently, that's improper. Apparently, that's a crime. I knew Mr. Bigdick. I tried to get him to touch me. I knew Mr. Bigdick. I tried to get him to fuck me. It was a total no-go. I knew Mr. Bigdick. Mr. Bigdick: He was an English teacher. Mr. Bigdick: He was a teacher first. Mr. Bigdick: He was a teacher last. When I heard about Mr. Bigdick, I just dropped fucking the three brothers Ng the next day, and cried. I like cum, I like cock, but Mr. Bigdick getting busted, for me, it was just too much. I may be a slut, I may be a whore, but so what. I've still got a heart. Maybe Mr. Bigdick's wife was a cripple, maybe he was too. They didn't matter; I was going to call him up.

Let me tell you about Mr. Bigdick. He had what most of us don't. Most of us count minutes, we count hours, we count days, we count years, we count time. We count it on the calender, we count it on the clock. Not Mr. Bigdick. He doesn't. He makes it. Time, Bettina, if we have it, it's only on the inside, where it counts, in the heart. It's no place else. That's why the *Wizard of Oz* works, he told me. Because Dorothy finds out that all time is within her; it's internal. Most of the movie depicts an external journey, but we learn that it's really all just internal. That, Bettina, is really the only place reality is. That is what Christ meant, Bettina. And when he said this, in the public classroom of America, he touched my knee. He put his bare hand on my bare knee. When Christ talks about the beginning being his end, the same thing as T. S. Eliot, when Lao Tzu says the nameless was the beginning of heaven and earth and speaks about the myriad creatures, it means the same thing. Reality is internal. In fact, Bettina, that's the only place it is. There is no other reality. There is no other world. The external world, he said, spreading his arms: Chimerical. It's a beast: A lion, a goat, and a snake. It's a monster. That's the external world. Unfortunately, we are frequently judged by that world and are undone by that world. Sitting here in the classroom with my hand on your knee, I am judged, if I were to be, by a world that condemns me. How many times would I wish, he said, to have driven you home? But the external world, the external eyes are always seeing us and watching us and judging us and counting us. Everything manifest in the external world eventually comes to be counted against us. That is why those who accumulate, or amass nothing in the external world look so hapless when they are eventually condemned by it. Such people, the Christs, the Buddhas, the shoeless beggars of the world create in the stead of manifest externalities, vast and beautiful internal worlds we scholars of reality name paradise or nirvana or sanctuary. It is the world even bitter Holden creates in the icy lagoon of Central Park. A lagoon. A lacuna. A lake. A pool. A gap. A place of nothing. Sometimes this is referred to, Bettina, as the Void. When they came for Christ at Gesthemane, it could have been Tuesday. It could have been Thursday. It could have been next week, next month, or next year. It really didn't matter. Days, weeks, hours, minutes, years, these are all really external measures again. Are you ready for life? Now that is a question worth answering. When you are, the world and all her being in every infinite measure of it is ready for you. And when you are ready, the day will come and you will be, too. The day, Bettina, the day. At any time of your life, you will be. The day.

That, people, was Mr. Bigdick, and why I called him. That, people, is who my Mr. Bigdick really was. Can you see why I really wanted him? Maybe not. I do. He was pretty weird. Pretty out there. He was a gem, a jewel. He was my Emerald, my Emerald City, my Emerald City divine. I really wanted him. I wanted him, you see, for myself.

I remember he said in class: Action isn't about a guy going into a shopping mall, pulling out a semi-automatic, and mowing everybody down. That isn't action. Why don't we see Oedipus pushing jewelry through his eyes? Why don't we see Jocasta swinging from the rafters with a noose around her neck? The internal motives from which these deeds spring, not the deeds themselves, are what is most important. That's action. And sometimes, he said to us, more often than we are aware is possible, like poor Oedipus, we find ourselves in situations that indeed try our characters;

these, our characters, are just our natural inclinations to choose one way or the other. Oedipus, his is a character that chooses to pursue his origins in the name of truth. Jocasta, hers is one that'd rather leave that alone. The action in the play, it makes total sense: To find the slayer of King Laius, to uproot the defilement of Thebes. That is what *praxis* is. Action. It is the well-spring of intention, the good cause, rational. The kind of stuff you're made of, how you perceive things, and your basic character, the interplay of these two things, he said, result in action. Action: It is not a drive-by shooting, he said. It is not the Indianapolis 500. It is what the poet Dante called "movement of spirit." I had a girlfriend once, he leaned back saying to all of us, who told me: *Just to be able to read Dante in the original is worth learning Italian for*. Action: Active. Thought and Character, both passive: The interplay of which makes you do what seems good to you. That's Action. That, he said, is *praxis*. These, folks, he said to us, are the basic tenets of Aristotle's *Poetics*, that famous little chapbook on How to Write Movies and Make Millions of Dollars from Them. These days will come for all of us, folks; these days will come for all of us. Later, he said to me alone, it's actually through studying the *reductum ad adsurdum* of literature that we can learn to navigate better the events that actually confront us and with which we are day by day confronted. We are bombarded by them. The daily interplays of life are infinitely complex; in cumparision to the daily buying of a cinnamon twist and a cup of hazelnut coffee from Anna, the woman at the cafeteria register, he said to me, James Joyce's *Ulysses* is a simple comic strip. We are infinitely deeper than any literature. Literature, he whispered, is only lamp-posts. Language, the light. Literature: Only the lamp-posts to spirit; not spirit. Language: Spirit itself, and we are spirit's vessels. Books, he said to me, just help us see where we've come from, what we are, and where the hell we're going. They're helpful because of the virtue that they are, thank God, Bettina, so reductive. Otherwise seeing through the murk is tough. Life, otherwise, a gigantic purple haze. A muddle. A blacked-out cave. Murk. They help us to see through the muddle. They help us achieve clarity elsewhere. And clarity, for me, for Aquinas, as we saw in *Portrait*, is quite key.

That's basically what he said. Obviously, it's not *verbatim*. I've obviously basically made it up. But what he was basically saying I've basically got and it basically makes sense. When you listened to Mr. Bigdick, he never was just talking about books. He never was just talking about Aristotle when he was talking about Aristotle, or Joyce. He was talking about himself, not himself himself, but what he knew, from his own life experiences. It was like he talked about them to teach us. That's why I wanted to do him. I wanted to be done by someone who was real. And he was real.

I really felt bad for him when I heard the news. I bugged him so much 7th period and even after school. It's no small wonder that he never pressed charges against me! I was basically asking for it. Gosh! I totally like harassed him. So, when I heard he'd been busted I was like no friggin way, not Mr. Bigdick. Not him. Please, don't be him. But it was, and this is what I found out. He ended up resigning. He ended up fired. He ended up going to jail. He ended up on probation. He ended up blacklisted. He ended up in the paper. He ended up banned. He ended up humiliated. He ended up reviled. He ended up being threatened. He ended up sued. He ended up invaded. He ended up attacked. He ended up ruined. He ended up shunned. He ended up doubted. He ended up, what difference does it make? All I know is he's not working at HHS anymore.

It was my last Spring break. My senior year, this one, at college was coming to an end. I was just finishing up with the three brothers Ng like I said, when Xsu-Xsu called me about Mr. Bigdick. I decided to go there. I knew really that he wasn't there, but I had to see it for myself. I had to see it with my own two blue Irish eyes that old Mr. Bigdick wasn't in his own classroom. That's the only way I'd believe it. You could tell me anything, but only till I didn't see him there at his old laminated desk in his old spinning dusty chair would I really really believe that old Mr. Bigdick was gone. So I went there. I couldn't even get in the school. They wouldn't let me in. They had security guards, and the same hall monitors I passed without a problem for years would not let me go past them. It was absurd. It was ridiculous. Like it was a war zone. I'm from here! I went here! I'm from Harrisford! I grew up here! My parents pay taxes! I'm a U.S. citizen! I'm sorry, honey, they said, if you're not a student, you cannot be on school premises without a pass. I tried to argue. It was pointless. I couldn't say I was going to visit a teacher who wasn't even there anymore! I couldn't say I was going to hopefully visit a teacher who was just busted for sexual harassment either. Is Mr. Bigdick, the former English teacher here who was charged with sexual harassment here? I'm a former female student of his, and I've come to visit him. I couldn't say that now, could I? Obviously! That would look ridiculous. I couldn't even be there. When I got there and they turned me away, the only smart thing I did do is not say who I was going to see. I'm sure they would have turned around and arrested me. I'm sure. Or charged him more times because of me. I'm sure if they really knew who I was, they'd have broken into my cumputer too like his and taken it. Can you imagine that? Can you imagine what that would have looked like? Can you imagine what my cumputer would have looked like in all the newspapers: BIG DICK STALKS STUDENT'S MEMORY IN HHS HALLWAY. Those would be the headlines about me and Mr. Bigdick from my old high school if they knew who I really was. They didn't. So I just went away.

# 16

## *Bigdick's last lessons*

Firemen becum arsonists. Cops becum criminals. Politicians becum crooks. Everybody knows that. And teachers becum pedophiles. It's all so obvious to me like robbing the bank because that's where the money is. People have their passions and you can't excuse them for it. I'm a writer, I just can't help lying. I do it pretty much all the time. Not lie lies. I'm always trying to tell the truth, really, I am. It's just when I put it down it comes out different, that's all. I know of this one writer and what he does he just writes and does what he's doing and when it's done says to himself if it's interesting or not. "And that's all," he says. That's pretty much how I am, too. His name was Philip Whalen and Mr. Bigdick talked about him. That's how I know about it. That's how I got my start. He gave me Yeats' *A Vision* to read, and he gave me *How to Do Things with Words* by J. L. Austin, and also *A Grammar of Motives* by Kenneth Burke. Honestly, they were way over my head at the time. I only read part of *How to Do Things with Words*, honestly, because I liked the title. It sounded like a kid's book, you know, one that would be fun to read. Trust me, it isn't! It jokes and stuff, but it gets very serious. Everything starts having all these subscripts and stuff and it's a pain to keep track of and follow. It's like all the rules you have to follow in calculus. I'm good at math, but I didn't like to do it. So, I don't. Not in college, I didn't. For a writer, these texts are more important than most of the other crap that's been written over the last hundred years. Wow! You should have heard him getting going about that! Talk about bugbears! Talks about peeves! Mr. Bigdick, let me tell you, he had a few. Why on earth, he'd go, would I want to read a book by someone with a brick face? Why do I want to read that? A brick face with no emotion telling one handful of preposterous made-up lies after the next? Why? It's like a cliché of unbelievable tall-tales both teacher and student contract to go through like a contract of clichés when said student makes up said stuff about said paper not being turned in for whatever said reason both know they aren't supposed to believe is true anyway. It's like bad art. It's like calling Norman Rockwell an artist. No, folks, he's an illustrator. He's a very good magazine illustrator, but, folks, let's stop there. Marquez is so vain and stupid, that's what Mr. Bigdick said, *vain and stupid*, he makes it a virtue to tell a story with a brick face, and goes on to pay homage to his grandmamma from whom he learned this ridiculous jail-house style of narrative lying. But that's not even the worst of it. The worst is that Marquez just invents and invents and invents all kinds of shit that doesn't exist. Oh, excuse me, it does exist: In the external world. His external world. But why do I want to know about that? Why on God's good earth would I want to know a page about some brick wallface telling me a story about a totally external world? You go to a supermarket. There are things on the shelves in the aisles from which to choose. You choose them. Maybe you've got a ton of shopping to do, and for some reason you go to the frozen section first and pull off a half gallon of Neapolitan ice cream. The reason you do that is important. The ice cream: An accessory to your latent motives now turned manifest in the, yes, external world. But the external world only illustrates and serves to illustrate what's going on inside you. In Marquez' supermarket, whatever the hand makes up is there to pull off the shelf. Magical? I don't think so. Real? I don't think so. It's just an arbitrary phantasmagoria of jungle bullshit that the rest of the so-called civilized world bows to because some Colombian peasant puts his wife in serious debt for what we East Coast thinkers think is sorta cute because its seems like some novel or autochthonous way *los campesinos* spin their jungle yarns or jungle vines or what have you in the jungle that we in our bourgeois ivory towers of monastic thinking haven't heard the likes of yet. But it doesn't mean that it's good. It doesn't mean that it has a point. It doesn't mean it has a value. Stamp: Nobel prize. Stamp: *Emperor's New Clothes*. I can't stand the stuff, Bettina, he said. I want to know what's going on inside people's minds, especially the mind of a writer. Marquez, he writes from that writerly, novelistic distance of, say, about an arm's length away from his work. You can literally see him at his desk making up this shit as he's making up this shit. You know the entire time your eyes are on the page that it is a novel you're reading. And you know the entire time your eyes are on the page that you are the reader reading that novel. You never forget that. You never forget either of those. It's like smoking a real pipe that has written on the side: *Ceci n'est pas une pipe*. But of course in that case it is. In Marquez it's the opposite. It's written from the vantage point that both writer and reader are supposed to take *One Hundred Years of Solitude* as real, but you cannot forget for one single syllable that it's totally fake, every second, all the time. In Marquez' supermarket everything on the shelves is made up. The aisles themselves dissolve to watercolor quaintness. The writing, the brush dipped in water of whatever comes to mind, disappears. *One Hundred Years of Solitude* is what Keats aptly distinguishes as the vital difference between Fancy, or whatever bubbles up involuntarily, and Imagination, what we actively work on and engage in through an act, hear the word *act,* of volition or will. Marquez, just a meaningless inert dreamscape. Yup! That was Mr. Bigdick for ya! Nothing quaint there! He was just the bravest, the bravest of them all. Good writers tell the truth, whatever that is, he said, because they can't help it. Bad writers lie, he said, because they can't help that. There are good writers and bad writers. There are good teachers and bad teachers. There are good cops and bad cops. There are good eggs and bad ones. I knew what kind of egg Mr. Bigdick was. They must have got him all wrong.

Mr. Bigdick, he had a style like nobody else's busines. One time this kid, Thurgood Morgan, he comes to class wearing this court jester type of flannel hat. It had bells all over it and you could hear the bells ringing halfway down the hallway. Every time he moved his head, the bells would go off. It was kind of like a Lappish hat from Lapland. And instead of just telling Thurgood to take it off, because every time he moved it did jingle, Mr. Bigdick joked about the delightful tintinabulation singing from Thurgood's head. Thurgood didn't know what he meant of course really; so, Mr. Bigdick nodded over to a fat green dictionary. *Tin-tin.* He wasn't mean or anything. He just wanted him to learn another word. The next day Thurgood comes back with the jester hat on again. *What's that sound I hear again ringing in my ears?* And Thurgood slides the Lappish hat off again: *Tin-tin-something.* It sure worked a lot better than yelling at him about all the noise he was making, which he was. Thurgood was a weirdo. So was Mr. Bigdick. It's not like they got on especially well either. Not all weirdos even like each other. Probably more the opposite. He just wanted him to learn about what he was doing. If anyone wasn't acting the way they should have been, it was probably us. There weren't that many hard and fast rules Mr. Bigdick kept. Not wearing hats in class was one of them. What Mr. Bigdick's vocab lesson was about was about telling Thurgood to take off his hat. It took him two days to learn the word and he didn't wear the jester hat to class anymore. And what else? He didn't let you eat in class or drink. *It ain't California*, he said, whenever somebody starting eating there. Whatever that meant. Whatever. No, it was pretty much us. I'd come in with a scoop neck that showed off the tops of my tits, they're pretty small ones anyway, and I'd never go to a job like that. Unless I was waitressing. There I would because tips go up the more you show. That's just common sense. But school is school. And what I'd wear, what we'd wear: Totally inappropriate 70% of the time. Heels to throw off your balance a little to give your ass more out-push. Skirts that flashed the color of your underwear every time you rounded a corner and blew up a flap. Stretch tops that pressed against your nipples so they'd bug out anytime. Underwear that was just a tiny thin strip a pink fabric running up the back of your ass. Chair food. You'd make sure that only that strip and the rest of your bare ass was showing when you sat. It was total whore-show, total like a Rio de Janiero runway as far as we could make it, as much as we could push it. Girls dressed to look fuckable and hot. Girls dressed to show off their tits and pussies. Face it, teenage ass in high school was totally unavoidable. We grew up on Condé Nast. Our world was totally like *Seventeen*, *Teen People*, and *Cosmo*. I mean what is Victoria's Secret? It's a whore shop. Everybody knows it. Everybody does it. Everybody works it. Girls, we're pumped up to fuck from the time we're like eleven. If you haven't fucked like about ten different guys by the time you're done with high school, you basically haven't passed the pool test. That's a gym requirement. Fucking in my book should be a graduation requirement. If you hadn't been fucked over and over by the time you got out of high school, you needed your head checked out by a real brain specialist or you had to have a pretty good reason like your boyfriend's Superman and he'd been turned into a quadraplegic by being thrown off a galloping thoroughbred race horse on Easter Sunday. Besides that, there's no excuse. It's just the culture we live in. It's pretty whorey. Getting pregnant, that's like getting a 5 or a 4 on your AP exam. Woo-woo! You've made the big time. Having the baby? Only losers do that. An abortion? That's totally Ivy League. You see, we were all out of control. The greatest job teachers do practically is keep their paws off us. What I'm saying is Mr. Bigdick was my Superman. And I kept myself for him. I was a real freak, quite honestly, not to be balling all the guys who wanted to do me. They thought I might be a lesbian. They thought I was a prude. How wrong they were there. I turned out to be a real anal freak actually! I love sex. I'm basically a sexaholic if there is such a thing. And Mr. Bigdick, it was like he really was crippled or something. He was a bit lascivious in his lustre, a bit crude in his verbiage, a bit fidgety with his fingers. But his eyes didn't go down my shirt. His words were never suggestive. And his hands never groped me. Fucker! I've said that before, haven't I? What a fucker, Mr. Bigdick! The best year of my life, poof! There it went, up in smoke! Not really, I'm just kidding. I've been fucked so much since then that it hardly matters. Him getting busted, what a joke. We should have been busted. The whole school should have been busted. It was a total

orgy. An orgy of tight clothes, loose language, and bad be-
havior. The whole school was. A total concupiscent carnival
of carnal desire. Some of us took off forty days for Lent. I
did. And trust me, there's nothing in the world sexier than
playing the role of a good Catholic girl who fucks hard on
the weekends and walks modestly down the hallway with
a soot cross on her forehead on Ash Wednesday. I know, I
played her. At least the modest part. No, there's one more
thing sexier than that: It's when a schoolgirl dresses just
like a schoolgirl. A tartan skirt. Tights. White. White blouse.
Patent leather shoes. Little brass buckles. I know, I played
her too. That's the total cock tease. And that's what we did.
That's what high school is. A gigantic cock tease. You put
out when you have to. You put out when you can. You put
out when you like to. Besides then, besides those times, high
school's a total cock teaser. That's the point of it mostly. To
tease guys' cocks. I chose the best cock in the whole school
to tease. I have a nose for that sort of thing. Mr. Bigdick's,
his smelled the best. His smelled the biggest. His was the
biggest bestest best- smelling cock in the whole school. Non-
pareil. I loved to smell it. Whoops! Am I supposed to feel
sorry for that? Did I invent the system? Did I set things up
to be that way? I am sorry for what happened to him, but
me, I am just a daisy in a field of daisies. I'm just a daisy in
a big, wide, open field of daisies. I'm not the only one. There
is a whole field of daisies. A whole field of us. Smell us, smell
us! Do daisies even smell? Oh well. I don't think so. But
we're American daisies and we all want to be fucked. Mr.
Bigdick, he just wouldn't. Mr. Bigdick, he just couldn't. No,
we fucked him. That's what I think happened. We fucked
Mr. Bigdick. It probably happens all the time.

## 17

### *Phone sex*

*Hello, Mr. Bigdick? Hello, Mr. Bigdick? It's me, Bettina.* That's what I said when I called him. I was concerned. I wanted to find out how he was. I decided even if Mrs. Bigdick answered I was going to call him. There was no reason not to. There wasn't anything between him and me. They were in the phone book. It is a free country. I wasn't trying to intrude. If he didn't want to talk to me I'd understand that. If she said he wasn't home I'd accept that. She was his wife. Even though she was an invalid. Even though she was Jewish. I wasn't going to hurt him. I really felt bad about what happened. I wanted him to know that I supported him. I wanted him to know that I wouldn't ever say a thing against him. I wanted him to know that I would never cross him. I wanted him to know I would never testify against him. Even if he did push a strawberry in my mouth. Even if he drive me home once. Even if he did put his hand on my knee once. Even if wrote me letters. Even if he sent me emails. I wouldn't say anything about him. I would never say a thing, anything against you, Mr. Bigdick. I wanted him to know that. Gosh! I was so wet just thinking about it, just thinking about calling him, I just hung up the phone and started jerking off thinking about it instead.

*Hello, Mr. Bigdick.* This time I really called. His wife, Mrs. Bigdick, didn't answer. I'm not sure she even exists. Whatever. Some things are made up and some things aren't and some things it doesn't really matter if they do or they don't. That's sorta the way I felt about her. Maybe she was, maybe she wasn't. It's like she didn't. I mean, she did have a name and Mr. Bigdick once talked about her and the *Christina's World* poster. But besides that, there was nothing. That's the only connection there was. That's it. Besides that, nothing connected Mr. Bigdick to missus anybody. So I called, and he answered. *Hi,* I said. He knew who I was right away. Not that I have a particularly distinctive voice or anything. It's just, you know, young. And how many young women like me were calling Mr. Bigdick at home? I sorta wanted to imagine dozens, to tell you the truth. I didn't want him to be so lonely. Imagine having sex with an invalid like once a week all the time. Yuck! That's gross. I'm sure he had to do something. But I didn't want to talk about Mrs. Bigdick. She doesn't exist. Right. *Bettina,* he said, in a soft voice like I'd never heard from him before, *it's probably not such a good idea for me to talk to you right now.* It was sweet and gentle, almost *pianissimo.* He acknowledged the trouble he had had. He sounded humble. Humbled. So little. So small. When I brought up what he'd said about *Oedipus Rex* and action and character and all that and how what makes a person is how he responds to situations in life that are often beyond his own control and how the best we can do in life is manage our situations whatever they be and how the biggest mistake anyone can make is to believe that one can control life and its outcums and how sometimes like Job the lot seems inordinately harsh and unjustly cast against him and that such a situation is like the nuclear testing ground of the human spirit and how even the baby birds in their nests their fresh baby-blue shells spilled to the ground never really ever know if their own mother and their own father is ever coming back and how even when life is like Carole King's tapestry of rich and royal hue from way back in the 60's to way in the future all of a sudden a deer can just jump out of the hedges and disrupt the whole thing and how we need to somehow find within ourselves the power to be grateful for what we have rather than harbor resentment for what we have lost and like Mr. Antolini says to live our lives for a good cause rather than die for a noble one and to keep also in mind that babies learn to smile and to return to being the uncarved block and how knowing one's adversary is no less if not more important than knowing one's friend and that in all things one must strive to keep the whole intact and if this is not possible then to do whatever one can to minimize losses — when I was talking to him about all the wonderful things we had shared both in class and out of class I was at the same time gently swirling my left index finger around and around my love-button around and around practically gasping by the end of it practically dying by the time I was through practically choking on my words practically suffo-cating practically smothered practically strangled practically dead swirling and swirling counter-clockwise my left index finger around and around on my reddened love-button. Oh, Christ! I talked about Sophocles, Thomas Hardy, Ar-istotle, Joyce, Conrad, John Berger, Ezra Pound, Lao Tzu, Sun Tzu, Goethe, Yeats, Keats of course, and Coleridge, too. All of them. I talked about all of them and jacked off the whole time smoothly while I was talking without Mr. Big-dick ever noticing it. *Bettina?* He said once, and I thought I was caught. I had paused of course and was biting my lip literally on the lip, trying to keep in my voice from cumming in the phone again as I already had a few times out loud. *Bettina? I was just thinking, Mr. Bigdick; I was just thinking,* I said. *I thought,* he said, *you'd lost me.* That was sweet of course: To have lost me. To have lost Bettina. No, Mr. Bigdick; you have not lost me. Ever. Ever. I have found you. And I came, and came, and came. He was really very unsure of talking to me; so I did most of the talking. I did most of the talking, and I did all of the cumming. Again, and again, and again. I was sorta hoping he was doing the same thing on his end actually. I was hoping he had pulled out his big red cock and was stroking and stroking it. To me. I gave him all the time to do it. I gave him all the space to do it. I gave him all the room to do it. I gave him all the world to do it. I imagined him with his big big red hard cock going in me, filling me up, and his smiling smiling eyes looking down at me. I pictured him and me chanting together *Western Wind*, just as he had inscribed it on the book he gave me together. Here it is, again:

> *Western wind, when will thou blow*
> *The small rain down can rain?*
> *Christ, if my love were in my arms*
> *And I in my bed again!*

And cumming together at the exact same moment, just as the word *again* in *Western Wind* comes out of our mouths, from our lips. Either that or something else must have happened because all of a sudden he told me he had to go. He either realized what I had been doing and spoke to get off, the phone, that is; or, he had cum and wanted to clean up his own spermy mess. It was so Schrödinger's Cat-like! I just didn't know which to believe! And I was terrified to death to ask him. I just couldn't. Both were happening: He had cum, he had not; the cat was dead, the cat was not. Both true. Both false. Mr. Bigdick was such an enigma! A real live one, like the cat in the box! He was in me and he was not in me. Well, somebody had to look down and see which it was, and then one of those would be not. And that somebody was not going to be me. I didn't want to be the one to look down at my own pussy and know it. I didn't want to look down at my own pussy and honestly know which one it was. It was so cinema verité. It was so Robbe-Grillet. I read that in college, on my own. It was so Kierkegaard. I read that in college, too, on my own. It was so like I don't know what it was like! Crazy! It was crazy and exciting and right and wrong! Just like flavors of ice cream mixed up together at the same time. And when I was done talking to him and cumming to him like five or six times, I asked him if I could call him again, and believe it or not, he said yes. *Yes!* He said *yes!* Mr. Bigdick said *yes.* Mr. Enright Bigdick, Jr. Wow! Then I knew he must have been jerking off with me too. There would have been no other reason for him to have said *yes* otherwise. He must have heard me panting. He must have heard me sighing. He must have heard me muffling. He must have heard me miffling. He must have heard my breath. This must have gotten him off. This must have made him go. This must have made him see. This must have made him want. This must have made him hard. This must have made him jerk. This must have made him pump. This must have made him cum cum cum! I had him, and he had me. It was a cum party! It was a cum-fest. It was long-distance. I did it on my plan, pretty late at night, so the minutes were free!

# 18

## *Rembrandt*

Now I'm never very serious, but when I am I like to be taken that way. You take Rembrandt and his second wife. You take his painting of her when she was like seventeen and he was fifty-something. Nobody's calling the child protection agency on him. Nobody's boycotting Rembrandt. He'd be lynched by a dogwood today. Everybody knows that. Sure, not everybody's Rembrandt, I know that, too. And definitely that's important. Like if he was just some fifty-something year old fat slob found in bed with a teenager I'd probably find something wrong there. Besides it being what I think is just gross, I'd have to know who the guy was, basically. And who the girl is too. I mean, is he really taking away from her, sucking her away from something in life, or is he giving her something real in it she maybe wouldn't have had if it hadn't been for him? Are we going to call Rembrandt and his life porno? Is he robbing the cradle? What I'm saying is, so what if there was something between Mr. Bigdick and me? Today everything's so professional this and professional that. Would it have been so bad? The guy knew a lot. Maybe he wasn't a total genius, but he was pretty far up the ladder. I've been with a lot of guys, so I know now what I'm talking about. There's a lot to learn from a guy like

Mr. Bigdick was. And there's a lot a guy like that could get from a girl like me. So what's wrong with that? Sure, it's not for everybody, but who's to decide what everybody does all the time? The law? Take John Donne. He married a girl who was like also in her teens too. He got thrown in jail by her father first, sure, but he did it anyway. He was just crazy for her. The famous line about it goes: *John Donne. Anne Done. Undone.* Sometimes, folks, you've just got to let a girl decide what to do. We know what cars we want to drive, we know what clothes we want to wear, and we know what guys we want to fuck. A smart guy who'll be faithful and makes you feel good about yourself over a guy your own age who'll disappear off to college and forget you ever existed? We know how to decide what's what and what we want. What was decided on Mr. Bigdick was what was good for him. Basically, he was undone. And the real serious part is he got undone for what's called conduct unbecumming a teacher. He was a teacher and was unbecum that. That's my word, by the way. Used like that. They unbecame him. Undid him. Really, what I'm trying to get at is it was mostly us whose conduct was unbecumming. My conduct was really unbecumming a student. I was trying to sleep with him. Let's face it. Plain and simple. And most students, let's face that: Their conduct is pretty unbecumming. Everything, the whole system worked to undo him. Mr. Bigdick, if anything, he was helping me to becum a student, and to be one. I never, even in college, learned so much about literature and life as I did from him. He didn't separate them into two piles: The pile of life here, and the pile of literature here. It's like in *The Great Gatsby* where Mr. Bigdick talked about seeing the night peppered with stars, and never seeing the night sky the same way ever again and how the sky informs the book and the book informs the sky and we are there to see experience have see both. Or like in Hitchcock's *The Birds*. After you see that movie the next time you see blackbirds perched on a telephone wire, or a murder of crows gathered in a tree, they don't look the same as they used to. They've becum malevolent, thoughtful, a little too conscious for my taste, he said. And sure, he'd talk about seeing the seagulls sitting on the rocks of the breakwater off the end of the beach when he was a kid and how after seeing *The Birds* in black-and-white on T.V. those seagulls were scary to him just sitting there, but that's the whole point. He made it personal. Which is what made Mr. Bigdick such a great teacher. Everything was a text. His life, his books, the movies, whatever came to mind became part of the text. It's like consciousness or being conscious. Text isn't artificial. Texts aren't artificial. They're real. They're the place where memories are kept, where life is put together and means something. We basically, unbecame him. And I was part of that.

I've never been a saint. I've pretty much proved that I think! I'm not an angel. I wasn't born with wings. I was like a closet. And you, Mr. Bigdick just being you, you opened me up.You opened up my closet. And there was so much in it, so much in my closet. I can't thank you enough. Once you opened it, I just kept opening and opening it up. And the more I opened up my closet, the more came out. I've had over a hundred thirty guys in my closet, and over a hundred thirty guys have come out. I'm going for 200 by the time I'm twenty-four. I've got some catching up to do. I mean, Lord Byron, in Venice alone, that guy fucked over two hundred pieces, he said. That's what he wrote. So if that guy did it in just one country, then so can I. Like I've said, I'm into sex, but I'm more into experience. Experience is the mother of all knowledge. That's an original. And if it's been said by someone somewhere else some other time, I don't care. Not that I don't care care; I mean, I don't claim credit for it. I don't need that, credit. Not for being orginal or not or anything. I'm just Bettina Lillemoore, a regular twenty-first century fox. I'm really not that pretty, but I don't care; I'm a fox. Meoww! Watch me roar. Watch me twist and turn and tumble and toss a metaphor! Woof! That's what Mr. Bigdick taught me the most that language is and language was made for.

I've had dozens and dozens of guys. And I plan to have dozens and dozens more. But maybe not starting tomorrow. Tomorrow I think I'll take the day off.

# Afterword

The sad circumstances of our Union today breed unique situations. One skips routinely over the headlines in which one more teacher is snared in a web of scandal and disgrace. One shakes one's head at the poor student, especially when that student is female, over her having been the classroom victim of sexual impropriety. Like pious monks in a cloister, the nation performs a silent collective clucking over the breach of the hallowed tradition of trust between yet another high school girl and her school's otherwise revered male teacher. (One never encounters these articles about any that are not.) Few things, in fact, evoke more disgust in the public's eye, than these sour relationships. Yet, however common they are, one almost never hears a word of remorse by either party involved in these tabloid scandals. Perhaps both parties are blighted? Perhaps both parties' characters are grievously flawed?

In her brisk and altogether brave début novel, which makes springtime as plain as the song of the robin, Ms. Lillemoore paints the pattern of pedagogical seduction not as anathema but integral to the healthy sort of "passionate" learning and teaching which, at the same time, the entire public seems also to be routinely cheerleading as absolutely vital to the long term public good and progress of society, not to mention the basic good of the nation's children. She does this barely letting the reader ever catch his or her own breath.

Let me be plain: The seduction of which I write is not one which constitutes fornication, but it is erotic all the same. It is an erotics not of a sex act, but one that does have everything to do with "the elating sensation of a physical carnation of one's body . . . the seductive effect of instantaneity between teaching and learning body," as Professor Erica McWilliams writes about in "Touchy Subjects." Rather than the Joy of Sex, Bettina Lillemoore paints a tableau of the Joy of Learning here which would make the likes of Simone de Beauvoir and Jean-Paul Sartre gasp for air together, and Henri Bergson's mystical reaching for his *élan vital* as graspable as the sticky, messy peach impotent Prufrock merely *thinks* about but is forever shying away from.

What is "won" by the one-time student in this novel is pleasure, both corporeal and intellectual, but never, at least with the teacher around which the novel revolves, a prize (or a price) that is actually sexual. It is the prize, hard-earned, long-lasting, that can only occur not in spite of but due to and because of the asymmetry of age, power, and even physical presence as gender. If *not* this, what we have is the three-dimensional space of a living classroom then collapsed into a two-dimensional area (but not a "space") of absolute neutrality, absolute predictability, absolute order, absolute paralysis, absolute torpor, and a near to next-to-absolute-zero zone of the possibility of any possible learning occurring between two human beings who, besides breathing in and out air, have all but disembodied themselves. The latter, conversely, is the danger of the American classroom today. Rather, this novel is all about seduction as the healthy component, if not *the* necessary ingredient for the very well-being of learning in the classroom.

At the same time, Ms. Lillemoore's novel qua memoir is clever enough never to explicitly indulge these themes—which would be a bore to have to endure any more than the several paragraphs I have written about them here. Rather, she embodies in her prose a fearlessness, a shamelessness, and a freedom of spirit that would tempt Zeus himself to loosen the shackles of Prometheus, rather than keeping that hero of humankind bound against a rock for his crimes against the gods. I proudly publish this book with the hopes that America not only hears but listens to these rapturous cries of literary freedom and inspiration. They are the cries of an Ophelia who does not drown in sorrow and shame and the true abuse of a courtly life that completely dulls and sterilizes her, but one whose voice rises above the confining castle walls of Denmark and reaches out to all the fecund world.

—Egbert Starr
March, 2015